THE DWELLERS BENEATH

Mary Arrigan

ATTIC PRESS
Dublin

First published in 1996 by
Attic Press
29 Upper Mount Street
Dublin 2

A Catalogue record for this title is available from the British Library

ISBN 1 85594 114 7

Cover Illustration: Angela Clarke
Origination: Attic Press
Printing: The Guernsey Press Co. Ltd

Attic Press receives financial assistance from the Arts Council/An Chomhairle Ealaíon.

<u>Dedication</u>

For Margaret, Linda and Teresa.

About the Author

Mary Arrigan is the author of several teenage novels including *Searching for the Green* and *Saving the Dark Planet* which are also published in the Attic Press Bright Sparks series. She also writes and illustrates the *Mamó* series and other picture books for An Gúm. In 1991 she won *The Sunday Times*/CWA Literary Award and in 1993 won the Hennessy Award for Best Emerging Writer. She lives in Roscrea, County Tipperary.

One

Miriam looked at the photograph which was printed on the back of the milk carton. HAVE YOU SEEN THIS BOY? asked the bold print over the freckled face of a little boy with a gap-toothed grin. There seemed to be a picture of a different missing child on the milk cartons every other week.

Miriam sighed as she closed the fridge door. Weird, she thought. Where could they be, those kids?

Her mother's voice wailed from the kitchen table; 'Miriam, you haven't eaten your cornflakes.'

'I'm not hungry, Mum.' Miriam pushed her lunchbox into her schoolbag.

Mrs Hobart looked helplessly at her daughter and wished she could find the right words to make everything all right. Miriam caught her look and forced a smile. 'Everything's cool, Mum. Stop the worrying.'

'Miriam ... '

'I'm all right, Mum. Please don't fuss. I've got to run. There's a history test.'

'Miriam, I know how hard it is for you. It's hard for all of us ...'

Miriam swung around. 'Mum!' she said impatiently. 'Please don't go on about it. So, we're here. We're stuck with it. We'll cope, you've said so yourself. Just ... please don't talk to me about it any more. Let's just get on with it. okay?'

'I only ...'

Miriam put her hand to her head. 'Mum! No more words. Please!'

She was out the door before her mother could say more. She pulled her jacket on over her sweater; she hadn't yet got used to the idea of not wearing a uniform to school. She sighed and longed to be back at St Elizabeth's. She longed for the security of the small, intimate convent school where she had attended every day since she was five years old. She longed for the familiar faces of old

5

friends and the clean smell of polished corridors. Order. Everything was so ordered at St Elizabeth's. Miriam liked order. You knew where you were at with order. Rows of girls, easy-to-relate-to girls. Boys were fine at discos and stuff, but not in the classroom. How could you open your mouth in a class where boys sprawled in graffitti-covered desks? How could you be part of a class discussion with open-mouthed yobbos sneering at anyone who followed the system by actually liking some school subjects? She wrinkled her nose as she looked along the row of modest houses and pulled the squeaky gate shut. She hated this neighbourhood. Why had they to move here? Why couldn't they have stayed where they were? Surely the bank could have done something to save Dad's business. Hypocrites. How well they'd fussed over him when his business was booming.

As a young man, he'd inherited the modest tailoring business from his own father and, within a few years, had increased the staff to eighteen. His name had spread and his list of customqers read like a *Who's Who* of big names. Hobart Handmades were the suits seen on media people, politicians and high-powered business people. Miriam and her brother Ed had been nurtured in a comfortable middle-class cocoon that left them ill-prepared for the sudden change in lifestyle. The bubble had finally burst. Miriam didn't know the full details; she didn't want to know. But she remembered the late night whisperings downstairs, the serious-looking men who came with brief-cases to the house and stayed until all hours. She remembered the clean rectangles on the wallpaper where pictures had once hung and the gradual disappearance of things like clocks and vases. And finally this. She shuddered as she remembered arriving here on a wet Saturday. She had fussed and wept loudly and sworn that she would never settle here.

For four days she had carried on so. Until one night, coming downstairs for a drink, she had seen her mother with her arms around Dad. He was crying. The scene would remain with Miriam for the rest of her life.

'We'll make a go of it,' Mum was saying. 'We'll survive, Peter.'

At that moment Miriam realised that she must grow up. Her childish selfishness had obliterated the fact that the people most hurt by the business crash were Mum and Dad.

After that she tried to settle in the new surroundings. If her parents could adjust, then so could she. Ironically, now that she'd become grown-up in attitude, her mother had entered into a guilt trip. At every opportunity she tried to justify everything to Miriam, getting herself into a knot of reasonings and explanations. Perhaps, Miriam thought, this morning's blow-out would help clear the air. Perhaps now Mum would just leave her to sort out her own head.

Two weeks ago Dad had got a job making ready-to-wear clothes in a factory. It was a terrible come-down, but he was positive about it.

'At my age,' he'd said, 'I'm fortunate to even get a job where I can use my skills. But ...'

'No buts,' Mum had interrupted him. 'You have a job. We have food to eat and a comfortable home. We have no needs.'

Miriam marvelled at her mother's practical strength and resolved to give this awful school her best shot.

'Life's a bitch,' she said aloud.

Looking back she saw a boy and girl who were in her form. Should she wait? If they proved to be unfriendly, she'd feel a fool. Better to pretend she hadn't seen them and keep going.

St Peter's was a good twenty minutes walk away, so she was surprised to see that the same boy and girl had got there before her. They must have got a lift. The boy looked at Miriam and winked boldly. Cheek!

Miriam tossed her cropped head and looked away. Dear God, please let the years pass quickly so that she'd be out of this dump. It wasn't that the teachers were so bad, it was the unfriendliness of the other students, and there were so many of them milling about the corridors. That was the worst of starting in mid-term; everyone had established friendships and she was an outsider. Well, see if she cared. There was probably none of them worth knowing anyway.

At lunch she sat on her own in a corner of the dining hall and unpacked the lunch she'd prepared the night before - brown bread and a slice of cheese. She grimaced - the hot chocolate in her flask was only luke-warm. Maybe if she didn't put the milk in. Maybe if she brought the milk in a separate container ...

'Do you mind if I sit here?' She looked up to see a moon face with glasses beaming at her. The boy they called Lou the Lick because he was always asking questions.

'Yes ... I mean sure you can ...' began Miriam, moving her chair to make room.

'If it wasn't so cold I'd have my lunch outside,' said Lou. 'I hate this crowded dining hall. It's all noise and steam and sweaty bodies. Is that all you're having for lunch? Birdfood I'd call that. Want one of my ham sandwiches? My Dad always makes too many. I think he's trying to beef me up into a muscle-bound riveter like himself. You don't need muscles to get on in life. It's up here you need it,' he pointed to his head. 'I intend using my superb brain power to make me a millionaire by the time I'm twenty-six.'

'Thanks. I don't like meat,' said Miriam, when she could get a word in.

'Oops, vegetarian are we? Against human nature that. Do you know that man started out as carniverous? Used to follow the herds of wild animals which he killed and ate. It was only when he discovered cereals that he began to stay in one place and eat wheat and stuff. Probably in a thousand years time ...'

Miriam laughed. 'Do you give lectures to just anybody or did you single me out?'

The boy grinned and looked at her over his glasses. His grey eyes were frank and humorous.

'I talk too much, don't I? I get it from my Mum. She never shuts up. Even when people walk away she keeps on talking.'

'Must be fun when you and she get together,' said Miriam, putting the crust back in the plastic wrapper.

8

'Sheer cacophony!' The boy threw his hands in the air. 'That means ...'

'I know what that means. I'm a very bright girl, actually. I know lots of big words like cow-pat and semi-colon.'

The boy pushed his milk carton to one side and put his elbows on the table. 'You're new, aren't you? I've been watching you.'

Miriam blushed.

'You keep very much to yourself,' Lou continued. 'You're either very shy or very odd. I don't think you're shy, so you must be odd.'

'Thanks a bunch!' Miriam laughed at his frankness.

'So, Lou the Lick has cornered Miss Snobbyboots.'

They both looked up. It was the boy who had winked at Miriam. The boy she sometimes saw on her own road. With him was the girl who always accompanied him. Snobbyboots! Perhaps she should be flattered.

'Well, if it isn't Hairy Harry, still in search of a brain cell,' Lou looked at Miriam. 'He's the only boy I know who causes excitement in the zoo. The apes think he's come home.'

'Stand up and say that,' Harry's eyes flashed.

'Harry, for goodness' sake drop it,' the girl was saying.

Lou stood up to his taller opponent. 'Certainly, my man,' he said.

'Take that remark back,' Harry put his hand on Lou's chest.

'Harry, will you have sense,' the girl pulled at his arm.

'Well actually I do take it back,' Lou simpered. Harry relaxed. 'It's not being fair to the apes,' added Lou. Harry's anger flared up anew. He pushed Lou against the table, knocking over the milk carton.

'That's tough talk from a little freak who's so scared of dogs he carries a gadget to chase them off.' He put his face up close to Lou's. 'Bow wow. Growwwlll.'

'My gadget, as you call it,' retorted the unruffled Lou, fishing a black whistle-like object from inside his shirt, 'is audible to mongrels and curs only. So, if I blow on it now, it will burst your eardrums.'

It took Harry a moment to recognise the insult and, when he did, he struck out at Lou.

'Harry, you great silly slob,' the girl pulled at his jumper. 'Can't you see you're acting like a fool. As for you,' she glared at Lou. 'You're as much to blame.'

'Me?' gasped Lou trying to wrestle his tie from Harry's strangling grip. 'He bloody started it.'

'Yes, but you needn't have led him on. You know Harry shoots his mouth off. You could have ignored him. Come on, Harry. Leave off.'

Miriam felt she ought to intervene. 'He did start it,' she said.

'Oh, what do you know?' The girl switched her attention to Miriam who wished she hadn't spoken. 'You're so stuck up.'

'Stuck up? Me?'

'Every morning you see us and you'd think we were invisible.'

'You're the unfriendly ...' began Miriam.

'Fight, fight!' went up the cry and a crowd gathered. The girl's fists waved as she tried to pull Harry back.

'That's it Harry,' a blocky youth with prominent teeth shouted. 'Do what your black sweetheart says.'

Harry's anger switched to the maker of that remark. 'Rourke!' he shouted. 'You racist pig. Come on. I'll take you on too.'

'Watch it,' someone cried, 'here's Mr Porter.' The crowd melted.

'What's the trouble?' Mr Porter looked glassily at the two boys. Harry was straightening his jumper and Lou was polishing his glasses.

'Trouble, Mr Porter? No trouble,' said Lou.

'I, er, I spilt my milk,' said Miriam, fishing some tissues from her bag and starting to mop up.

'And I'm just helping her,' said Harry's friend. They both disappeared under the table. Harry's friend caught Miriam's eye and they both began to giggle.

'Well, you know the penalty for fighting,' said Mr Porter, lamely.

'Fighting?' said Lou, putting on his glasses and peering innocently at the teacher. 'Us fighting?' The two girls under the table pressed their hands to their mouths to stifle their giggles.

'We were helping to mop up,' said Harry.

'Humpf,' Mr Porter stalked off, trying to look like he'd solved a major crime. The girls emerged from under the table. The four regarded each other sheepishly.

'You could have got me into trouble,' said Harry. 'It's what I would have expected from a little wimp.'

'Harry, shut up,' said the girl.

'I know. It was tempting,' Lou grinned. 'But, with your record for trouble you'd probably have been kicked out. Then I'd have no one to insult.'

'You weren't so bad yourself,' Harry's friend said to Miriam.

'For a snob,' said Miriam. They laughed and broke the awkwardness.

'I'm Latisha,' said the girl. 'Harry lives next door to me.'

Two

That evening, after school, Miriam was pleased to see Latisha and Harry waiting for her on the front steps. Latisha grinned, her strong, white teeth almost too large for her small face. Her hair was painstakingly beaded with multi-coloured wooden beads which swayed as she moved her head. Purple leggings showed off the shape of her long legs which seemed too fragile to bear the weight of the black Doc Martens which encased her feet. Over her red shirt she wore a white cotton jacket with purple patch-pockets.

'We'll show you the short-cut we take,' said Harry, ambling along beside the two girls. His long, loping stride made him seem skinnier and his jerky movements reminded Miriam of a puppet on a string. The image on his Megadeth t-shirt was worn and faded. Over it he wore a grubby, fake leather jacket with a Harley Davidson motorbike emblazoned on the back of it. His hair was short and stubbly, making his head look bony.

There was a hole pierced in one earlobe, but there was no stud in it. In another place, at another time, thought Miriam, she wouldn't be seen dead in the company of a guy like Harry. But somehow she felt comfortable with him. She liked the easy way of himself and Latisha.

'Look,' said Latisha pointing to a poster on a telegraph pole outside the school. 'Another kid missing.'

'That makes about eight over the past few months,' said Harry. 'What sort of pervert takes kids like that?'

'They can take my ratty brother any time,' said Miriam. 'He's just pure trouble.' She didn't really mean it, of course. Of the whole family Ed was the one who was least fazed by the change of lifestyle. He liked the squeaky gate and the cluttered back garden. Most of all he liked playing football on the small green with other kids - a pleasure previously unknown to him in the loftier atmosphere of suburbia.

They looked up at the poster of the missing child. There

was general concern at the disappearance of these children, all aged between seven and ten. The police had been to the school several times asking if anyone had seen anything suspicious and warning youngsters to report people who might be chatting up younger children.

'My Gran says that trust is disappearing,' said Latisha. 'People are going to be so suspicious of one another that no one will speak to anyone else. The world will be peopled by hostile and suspicious dummies; she says that homes will become fortresses and folks won't even know their neighbours.'

'Well, hasn't she got a posh way with words, your old Gran,' said Harry. He opened his eyes wide. 'We'll become a race of zombies.' He stretched his arms out in front of him and walked stiff-legged. 'Do not approach me,' he said in a monotone. 'Do not speak to me. Do not make eye contact with me. I am an island.' The girls laughed and ran after him.

'I think I'd prefer to take my chances with the rest of the human race,' said Latisha.

They came to a vacant lot with crude hoarding around it. This whole area of the street was due for re-development and, with its knocked and crumbling buildings, it resembled a mouthful of bad teeth. Between the graffitti and old posters there was a loose plank.

'Here we are,' said Harry, pulling back the plank to allow the two girls through. 'This is our short-cut.'

'So, this is how you get to school before I do,' said Miriam. 'I wondered about that. What is this place? It looks like no one has been here for years and years.'

The site was bigger than one would have imagined from the outside. It stretched right across to the street which ran parallel to the one they'd just left. The high walls of derelict houses looked down with sightless windows and, on the cropped walls of some of the ruins, you could see the marks where fireplaces and staircases had once been. Here and there faded wallpaper bore witness to years of habitation. The ground, where once there were floors that throbbed with footsteps, was now covered with high

13

clumps of nettles and prickly grass.

'I heard my father say that several property developers wanted to buy this space, but there's some problem about ownership and deeds and stuff. They can't locate the original owners or something. I hate the place,' Latisha said as she gave a dramatic shudder. 'It's got a bad ... a bad aura. But,' she then laughed, 'it sure cuts a chunk off our journey to school.'

Miriam gazed at the sad remains of a distant past. 'Isn't it hard to imagine that people once lived in these places?'

'Yes,' agreed Latisha. 'Choosing their wallpaper and lighting cosy fires.'

'Having afternoon tea and sewing patchwork quilts.' Miriam dropped her schoolbag and danced in the long grass. 'And waltzing in the parlour with dreary looking young men with hairy side-locks.'

'Not being allowed to vote or have a career,' Latisha put her hands on her hips. 'Who'd want to live like that?'

'Oh, I don't know,' said Miriam dreamily. 'You could marry some wealthy old codger and then have a passionate affair with a poet.'

'You should be so lucky,' laughed Latisha. 'You'd probably be an under undermaid, up at five in the mornings to light fires and take tea to the gentry.'

'Come on, you two,' called Harry. 'This place gives me the creeps.'

'You're right,' Miriam picked up her schoolbag. 'It *is* eerie. It's as if ... as if all those old houses are listening to us. They seem to be waiting ...'

'Come on,' Harry called again. 'Latisha, move your ass.'

'Big ignoramus,' retorted Latisha. 'Let's go,' she said to Miriam. 'I'm starving.'

'Me too,' said Miriam, and they both ran towards Harry.

'Hey!' Harry was crouching to look at something on the ground. 'What have we got here?' As he smoothed back the long grass, the sun glinted on the shiny object that had caught his attention.

'It seems to be a medallion of some kind,' said Miriam.

14

Harry picked it up and the three of them examined it. It was a circle of silver with a complex design on it.

'They look like leaves twisted around one another,' Latisha traced the pattern with her finger. 'Like the designs you see in old-fashioned books. Art nouveau, isn't that what they call it - Victorian sort of frilly designs.'

'It's very pretty,' said Miriam. 'Is it a brooch?'

'Looks more like a pendant,' said Latisha. 'See, there's a sort of loop for a chain. Careful, the edge is sharp - as if it's been worn for years and years ...'

'Could be magic,' laughed Harry, taking it from her. 'If I rub it, perhaps a genie might appear and grant me three wishes. Would you girls like to come to the Bahamas with me?'

'Sure,' said Latisha. 'Will you whistle up a load of fancy gear to wear as well?'

'There's some sort of writing on it,' observed Miriam, squinting at the unusual pendant. 'See? Funny symbols around the side.'

Latisha took it back. She gave an involuntary shiver. 'Heaven knows what it is or what sort of weirdo might have owned it,' she said. 'I don't like the look of it. It looks like some cult thing ...'

'Oh, listen to Miss Psychic,' grinned Harry. 'You read too much about occult rubbish, Lat. Get a life. This thing might be worth money ...'

'Leave it, Harry,' Miriam was surprised at Latisha's sudden snappiness. 'Don't mess around with found stuff.'

'It could be solid silver ...' persisted Harry.

'I said leave it!' Latisha's mouth hardened into a straight line and she threw the medallion into the long grass.

'Ah, jeez, Latisha,' groaned Harry. 'You didn't need to do that! I could have got good dosh for that.'

'Yeah, sure.' Latisha's dark eyes flashed. 'And maybe AIDS as well.'

'You can't get AIDS from ...'

'If you cut yourself with it, you could,' retorted Latisha. 'Anyway, leave it be. Come on.'

Harry gave a wry glance towards the bank of grass

where the pendant had landed.

'You're a fruitcake, Lat,' he said. 'You know that. A nutty fruitcake. I'm going over there to fetch it back.'

'It's you're the fruitcake,' Latisha thumped his arm. 'I got bad vibes from that thing and I don't want you messing with it.'

Miriam was surprised at Latisha's display of protection towards Harry, but she said nothing. After all she was just beginning to get to know both of them.

'Well, I'll come back for it,' muttered Harry. 'You'll see, I'll either sell it or get a huge reward ...'

'Oh forget it,' said Latisha. 'All you ever think about is how to make a fast buck. Come on.' She skipped ahead and the other two followed her across the eerie, lengthening shadows in the derelict place.

Three

Mrs Hobart was holding a pink letter in her hand when Miriam came down late to breakfast next morning. Dad had already left with Ed, whom he dropped off at the primary school on the way to work.

'Look,' she said, waving the letter at her yawning daughter. 'It's from your Aunt Ruthie. Her eldest girl, Sally - the one with the degree and the long hair - is getting married. A doctor she landed herself. That's what comes of working hard.' Mrs Hobart pushed the cornflakes towards Miriam. 'You get a good job and meet people worth knowing.'

Miriam smiled and poured herself some tea. Her words to her mother yesterday morning had obviously made a mark; much of the tension was gone from Mum's face and there had been no further attempts at reasoning out things. Maybe now things would return to normal between herself and her mother.

They had always got on well. Mrs Hobart, like Miriam, had brown eyes and dark hair. Both of them tended to be slightly plump. But, whereas Miriam simply looked well-filled out and older than her fourteen years, Mrs Hobart's roundness was a diet pusher's dream. There was always some faddy paperback in with the cookbooks. The rest of the family would sigh with relief when the fads were short-lived and Mum would return to her normal, bubbly self, eating doughnuts and Crunchies.

'And make a good match with a respectable bore,' Miriam laughed at her mother's remark. 'Then spend the rest of your life in a detached show house driving your snotty kids to ballet and fiddle lessons. Oh, Mum. I intend having a really good time. I'm going to join a heavy metal band, get a tattoo and live with a biker.'

She was glad to see a spark of her mother's usual good humour return. Mrs Hobart threw up her hands in mock horror.

'And make me a Hell's Granny! Thanks a bunch,

17

daughter.' She pointed to the letter in her hand and continued, 'anyway, they want your dad to do the tailoring for the wedding and have asked the two of us up to stay for the weekend - you know, to discuss styles and take measurements and things.' She looked across at Miriam. 'I'll ask your Aunt Edie to come over and stay with you and Ed.'

Miriam groaned. 'Oh, Mum. Not Aunt Edie. She'll make all kinds of stupid rules and have us in bed at some unearthly hour. Please!'

'Shush,' said Mrs Hobart. 'She's a good woman. She'll look after you well and she's a great cook. Not up to my standard, of course, but you won't starve.'

'Mum,' Miriam persisted. 'She's a crotchety old windbag. She'll make us miserable. She'll look around this place and tut-tut about how we've come down in the world.' She bit her lip, wondering if she'd gone too far. 'It would get heavy, Mum. We're making a new start; we don't need Aunt Edie to stir up things. I'm absolutely capable of looking after Ed and myself. Honestly.'

Mrs Hobart looked doubtful and, for one glorious moment, Miriam thought she was going to give in. Then she folded the letter and put it in her pocket. 'No,' she said. 'I couldn't rest easy if I thought you were here on your own. Not with all those weird things going on nowadays, youngsters disappearing and whatnot. No, I'll call your Aunt Edie this very morning and you'll just have to put up with it. That's that.'

'You're cruel,' said Miriam. 'I'll report you for exposing your loved ones to a hag.'

Mrs Hobart laughed and hit out at Miriam with a tea towel. 'Get out, you cheeky brat, or I'll ask her to stay for a month to put manners on you.'

Miriam sighed another of her well-perfected sighs as she closed the door after her. What a prospect for the weekend; Aunt Edie with her ill-fitting false teeth and her notions on how youngsters should behave - not to mention her endless stories about when her perfect Alice and David were children. She was really Miriam's grand-aunt, Dad's

18

mother's sister, so she was extra old.

Miriam looked up the road to see if Latisha and Harry were coming, but she wasn't surprised not to see them as she was rather late. Even so, she didn't take the short-cut through the derelict site. Not on her own, she wouldn't.

There was some excitement around the school when she arrived. A police car was parked outside and a crowd had gathered. Probably about that missing child, thought Miriam. Drawing near, she saw Latisha's tense face as she spoke to one of the policemen. She looked relieved when she saw Miriam approaching.

'Oh, Miriam. It's Harry. He didn't come home last night. His mother rang me late ...'

'Are you a friend of the missing boy?' asked the policeman, switching his attention to Miriam.

'Of Harry's? Yes, I'm a friend of his.'

'And when did you last see him?'

'Yesterday. We ... the three of us went home together.'

'Was he in some sort of trouble?'

Latisha interrupted before Miriam could answer. 'He wasn't in any trouble,' she said with a touch of anger. 'You people are always ready to slap accusations on the likes of Harry. He wasn't in any trouble.'

'Take it easy, sweetheart,' said the policeman. 'Only doing my job. We've had a spate of kids disappearing, but this is the first teenager and we have to investigate all possibilities.'

'Next you'll be saying that Harry kidnapped the kids,' said Latisha.

'Keep your cool,' said the policeman. He looked at the assembled youngsters. 'If you hear anything, anything at all,' he said, 'be sure to contact us.' But he knew he would hear nothing. There were never any clues in these disappearances. One or two people mentioned seeing shadowy figures, but there were always crazies who see shadowy figures everywhere. And that's what all this amounted to - chasing shadows. Same as nine or ten years ago when he had newly joined the force. At that time a number of small babies had disappeared over several

19

months. No trace was ever found. Now this. The public were naturally angry. Tempers were frayed in the police station as increasing pressure from High Up had them all in turmoil. He got into his car wearily and drove away.

At assembly, Mrs Hagerty, the headmistress, talked to the pupils about Harry and asked for any assistance in locating him. Nobody really paid much attention. In the first place they'd had this talk so many times now about kids who had gone missing that there was no shock any more and, in the second place, Harry was a known truant anyway, though he'd never gone so far as to skip from home. Still, it had just been a matter of time before he did that. 'A lost cause,' Mr Carr from Geography called him.

At lunchtime Miriam and Latisha met up with Lou on the Science Room steps. He echoed the girls' concern over Harry.

'I can't think where he might have gone,' said Latisha. 'I know for a fact that he has no money.'

'Has he relatives around?' asked Lou. 'After all it's not as if he's been gone for days. He might just have gone to a relative for the night.'

'He only has an uncle who owns a junkyard on the far side of town. His Uncle Jim. They can't stand each other.'

'What about his Dad?' said Miriam. 'Where is he?'

Latisha laughed scornfully. 'Him! He walked out on Harry and his Mum years ago.' Her face expressed concern again. 'Poor Harry. I feel so helpless. I wish there was something I could do.'

'I understand, Latisha,' Lou said gently. 'I know he's ... he's special for you, but I do think you're worrying unnecessarily. Harry's cool. He's not some gullible kid. He's streetwise. Could he have had a row with his old lady or something?'

Latisha nodded. 'They row a lot,' she agreed. 'Sometimes he threatens to leave and sometimes she threatens to leave. They're for the birds, the pair of them.'

'See,' said Lou, with a note of triumph. 'That's all it is. He's holed up somewhere in a huff to give his Ma a jolt.'

'Could be, I suppose,' began Latisha doubtfully.

Miriam nodded. She too felt that Latisha was being unnecessarily concerned. After all Harry was only missing since yesterday evening. She'd read of kids who disappeared for days on end and then arrived back cheeky as ever. But she suspected that the spate of child disappearances had caused Latisha's concern.

'Sure,' she tried to console Latisha. 'That's probably all it is, Latisha. He'll probably lope over to your house this evening, brassy as you like.'

'Tell you what,' Lou patted Latisha's arm. 'Give it until tomorrow. If the wretch hasn't clocked in by tomorrow, well ...'

'Well what?' asked Latisha.

'Well, we'll do something. We'll start searching.'

'We will?' Latisha's face brightened.

'Yes,' put in Miriam when she saw that Lou's suggestion was bringing some relief to Latisha's face. 'The three of us will start a search tomorrow. Lou's right. There's no point in getting our knickers in a knot just yet. Give it until tomorrow.'

Four

The next morning, Friday, Mrs Hobart fussed and bustled.

'I've left enough food cooked for yourselves and Aunt Edie,' she was saying. 'You put it in the microwave yourself, Miriam. Your Aunt Edie doesn't know how to manage modern things like that. She'd blow the kitchen apart. And don't forget to ...'

'For heaven's sake, Doris,' Dad said impatiently from the doorway, a travel bag in each hand. He'd managed to get the day off to set off early. 'We'll only be gone two days. Edie will be here in the afternoon. Let's get a move on before the weekend traffic starts. So long, Miriam. Keep your noses clean and keep the Heavy Metal decibels down low.'

Mum hugged Miriam and ushered Ed into the back of the car. Miriam knew that Mum would prefer to be taking Ed the whole way rather than just dropping him off at school. She often thought that her mother babied Ed too much, but she'd had two miscarriages before he came along, so he was a bit special. Miriam felt the need to balance things out, so she spent a great deal of time growling at her young brother.

She locked the door and put the key under the third geranium pot where Mum had told Aunt Edie to find it. Looking up, she spotted Latisha. How lonely she looked without Harry prancing about. Miriam waved and waited for her.

'Still no sign?' she asked.

Latisha shrugged her shoulders and shook her head. 'His Ma is in bits. She thinks he's run away because she didn't have enough time for him. She sits around all day feeling guilty and talking of giving up one of her jobs. Bit late for that,' she added mysteriously.

They took the usual short-cut through the derelict site. It seemed all the more eerie without Harry's loud banter to banish the haunting dreariness.

The schoolday seemed long and heavy. None of the

three friends felt much like fun and they talked at length about Harry's disappearance.

'I was so sure he'd be back by now,' said Lou. 'I really was, Latisha. Perhaps he is with that uncle,' he added hopefully. 'You know, the junkyard one.'

'Junk and other stuff,' said Latisha scornfully. 'Sometimes he pays Harry to deliver things for him. I figure they're hot goods. I keep telling Harry he'll get nicked if he's caught with stolen stuff. He said he'd lay off all that and I thought he had. Anyway, he's not there. Harry's mother rang the uncle and he said he hadn't seen Harry for months. He just laughed and said that Harry reminded him of himself, that he ran away at that age too. Fat comfort that was to Harry's Ma.'

'What about that derelict site?' asked Lou. 'You know, the place where Harry found that medal thing you told me about. Could he be hiding out there?'

'We passed through there this morning,' said Miriam. 'We didn't notice ...'

'But we wouldn't, would we?' Latisha brightened. 'There are lots of ruined houses where he'd shelter. Besides, if he was there he'd have been snoring at that hour. Let's make a start there.'

'Better not set too much hope on that,' said Miriam cautiously, afraid of Latisha's disappointment if Harry didn't prove to be there.

'But at least it's a start.'

There was a steady drizzle as the three friends made their way to the waste lot after school. The thin curtain of rain only served to make the atmosphere even more miserable. The long grass clung wetly to their legs.

'You girls do the ground-level ruins,' said Lou, with an air of authority that always seemed more credible when it came from someone wearing glasses. 'I'll climb up to the higher floors. Better leave my bag down. And this, my art project,' he dramatically tapped a large binder which was too big to fit in his schoolbag. 'This is five weeks' research on the life of the painter Raphael. I've to finish it tonight and read it for the whole class tomorrow. If anything happens this, old Sepia Tint will strangle me.'

'Sepia Tint?' Miriam raised her eyebrows.

'Ms Randall, the Art teacher,' laughed Latisha. 'She's old, about forty, and she always wears brown like those old-fashioned photographs you see in Victorian albums. Sepia tint - get it? Look, Lou,' she pointed to a niche in a low, ruined wall. 'Put it there and cover it with this bit of board. There,' she wiped her hands on her skirt. 'That will keep it dry while we search.'

They wandered around the site, climbing through half-boarded windows, calling out for Harry. Rats scurried under the rotten floorboards and old cobwebs brushed against the girls' faces as they stepped gingerly into decaying rooms.

'No sign,' sighed Latisha when they had done the whole round of the site. 'He's definitely not here.'

'We've certainly made enough noise,' said Lou. 'If he was here he'd have heard us. He'd have no reason to hold out on us.'

'It's no use,' Latisha shook her beaded hair. 'We might as well go home before we get soaked to the skin. He's not here.'

'Sorry, Latisha,' said Lou, retrieving his schoolbag from the wet grass. 'It was just a hunch that didn't pay off. Let's try somewhere else tomorrow.'

'If he doesn't come back in the meantime,' put in Miriam.

'Sure,' agreed Lou. But there was doubt on all three faces as they climbed back onto the street. 'Ring us, Latisha, if you hear anything.'

Latisha nodded. The two girls watched as Lou swung his schoolbag onto his back and set off down the shiny, wet street.

'Come on, Latisha,' said Miriam. 'We can't do any good hanging out here. Go and see Harry's mother when you get home. She might have news.'

'Yeah, you're right,' Latisha turned around. 'Let's go.'

An evening breeze swished across the wet grass in the derelict place, shifting the piece of board that covered Lou's forgotten art project.

When she reached home, Miriam was surprised to find Ed sitting on the step outside the back door, his schoolbag at his feet and his face miserable.

'Why are you sitting out here, you daft kid?' asked Miriam. 'Why aren't you inside with Aunt Edie?'

'She's not there,' Ed replied.

'Not there?' Miriam looked through the kitchen window. 'Perhaps she's upstairs. Did you knock loudly?'

'I banged and banged and even kicked at the door. Look, you can see where I kicked it. And she didn't answer. I'm telling you she's not there. Or else she's lying dead inside with her brains all spilling out ...'

'You disgusting brat,' said Miriam. But she was concerned. It would be most unlike Aunt Edie to let them down. She looked under the geranium pot and found the key, just as she had left it. There was no doubt about it - Aunt Edie had not been here. When she had let herself and Ed in, she went over to the phone. Mum would have a fit if she thought that the two of them were on their own. She dialled Aunt Edie's number. The phone rang for a long time at the other end before she heard it being picked up. A wheezy, out-of-breath voice said 'Hello'.

'Aunt Edie, is that you? This is Miriam.'

'Oh Miriam,' wheezed the unfamiliar voice. 'This is Mrs Peters, your Aunt Edie's neighbour from downstairs. Your aunt has had a bit of an accident. Hold on and I'll bring the phone over to her. Don't go away now.'

Miriam could hear the clatter of the phone and the wheezy conversation Mrs Peters was having as she moved it. What could have happened to Aunt Edie? Well, she couldn't be too bad if she was at home and able to speak on the phone.

'Hello, Miriam?' More clanking and clattering. 'Miriam, is that you, love?'

'Yes, Aunt Edie. What's wrong? Mrs Peters said you had an accident. Are you all right?'

'Oh, the most stupid thing,' said Aunt Edie. 'I fell down the last three steps on my way out to your place this morning. Only that Mr Peters found me and got me back to my flat I could be lying dead. His wife is here with me now. I'm terribly sorry, Miriam. The doctor said I'd be laid up for a few days. He said I was on no account to put weight on the ankle. I tried to ring your mother, but she had already left. Isn't this a nice howdy-do?'

'Don't worry, Aunt Edie,' Miriam consoled her. 'We'll be all right. You just concentrate on taking it easy. Ed and me will manage fine.'

'No, no. You can't stay there on your own, dear. These are terrible times. You must get a bus to here and stay with me for the weekend. Bring sleeping bags. I wouldn't rest easy if ...'

'Not at all, Aunt Edie' - perish the thought - 'I'll manage fine. I'll lock all the doors and windows.'

'No, dear,' persisted the old lady. 'Your Mum has charged me with looking after you and I will do just that, sprained ankle or no.'

She was spluttering now and Miriam could imagine her false teeth wobbling and almost feel the spray of spit from the other end of the phone.

'Aunt Edie,' she broke in on her aunt's martyred ramblings. 'There won't be a problem. I'll simply get a schoolfriend to stay with me. I promise.'

She could hear Aunt Edie discuss this proposition with Mrs Peters. After much muttering, she spoke again. 'Well, if you think that will be all right ...'

Miriam smiled with relief. 'Of course it will. I have a very good friend who will be delighted to stay with me. We'll be able to do our homework together,' she added for good measure. 'So, you can relax happily.'

'It's not my happiness that's in question,' sighed Aunt Edie. 'It's my duty to you and Ed ...'

'Oh, Aunt Edie. I promise we'll be fine. What can go wrong with two of us here with Ed? Anyway it's only for two nights.'

'Well, I'll ring every day,' said Aunt Edie. 'And if there's any problem, you'll contact me straight away?'

'I will,' agreed Miriam, wondering what on earth an old lady with a sprained ankle could do if there was an emergency.

'Very well then. Be sure to lock up.'

'I'll do all that. Take care, Aunt Edie. Relax and don't worry.' She put down the phone and whooped '*Yes!*'

While Ed set the table for the two of them, Miriam pondered over ringing Latisha. Up to now she had sworn that she would never ask anyone back to the small, council house. She could never envisage any of her old friends from St Elizabeth's feeling comfortable in these surroundings. Even in the wealthy decor of her old home, she'd always felt it was under scrutiny by schoolmates who visited. She'd always felt a need for new stuff to make her room come up to their expectations.

Still, she sighed, she'd liked her friends and missed them. That competitiveness was just a way of life with them. Strange how values change, she mused. She picked up the phone.

'Sure, I'd be delighted to come over for the two nights,' said Latisha. 'Gets me out of my weekend chores.'

'Great,' laughed Miriam. Except for the shadow of Harry's disappearance, this could be a good weekend after all. Miriam still believed that Harry would pop back into their lives as though nothing had happened.

'Can't I have a friend round too?' asked Ed.

'I'll have enough to do in looking after you,' replied Miriam. 'The last thing I need is another snot-nosed kid to mind.'

'I wish you'd drop dead,' muttered Ed. 'You're a fat bossy-boots and you make me sick.'

'Finish the table and try not to get up my nose,' said Miriam. 'And eat your dinner quickly. I want to get the things cleared away before she comes around.'

'In case she wants some of your dinner?'

'No, smart ass. Because I wouldn't want any friends of mine to think I live in a pig sty.'

'Oink, oink,' laughed Ed.

'Oh, belt up, Ed. You're a bore and I wish I didn't have to look after you.'

Five

'You came by taxi?' Miriam's eyes were wide with surprise as she opened the door for Latisha. Latisha laughed as she waved to the driver.

'It's my Mum,' she said. 'She drives for an all female taxi firm. She's on nights this week so she dropped me off.'

'Cool,' said Miriam.

'I have a video,' Latisha put it on the hall table as she took off her jacket. 'I'd got it out for myself anyway, so I brought it along.'

'Can I watch too?' Ed trotted into the hall, his red hair plastered flat after Miriam had made him wash the football mud from his face.

'It's for fifteens,' said Miriam, hanging up Latisha's jacket.

'You're only fourteen,' retorted Ed. 'I'll tell.'

Miriam sighed one of her 'martyred me' sighs. 'Meet my darling brother Ed,' she said to Latisha.

'Hi,' said Latisha, smiling at Ed. 'I have a brother just like you.'

'Why didn't you bring him?' asked Ed.

'Well, he's gone to stay with his Gran for the weekend,' she said. 'But I will bring him next time. I promise.'

Ed switched his attention to Miriam. 'What am I supposed to do while you're watching that stupid video?' he pouted.

'Oh Ed. Do you have to be such a pain ...' began Miriam.

'Do you play Cluedo? Latisha asked him, noticing the game stacked under the hall table.

Ed's face lit up. 'Yes,' he said. 'Can you play?'

Latisha laughed. 'Of course. Do you have the game?' She winked at Miriam who was about to protest. Playing stuffy games with her brother was not what Miriam had in mind for the evening. As Ed fetched the game and carried it into the living room, Latisha whispered in Miriam's ear.

'A quick game will make him happy and get him off our backs.'

Miriam smiled. 'You should be in politics,' she said.

'I intend to be,'said Latisha.'After I do my law degree.'

Miriam looked at her sharply and Latisha laughed.

'I know what you're thinking,' she said. 'You're wondering how anyone from St Pete's could think of a career like that.'

Miriam looked sheepish. She had never expected to find brainboxes like Latisha and Lou and many others among the pupils of St Pete's. In trying to adjust to the culture shock of a huge mixed school, she was only now beginning to find out that intelligence had little to do with class.

'Well, come down from your ivory tower, honey,' Latisha said good-naturedly as she followed Ed into the living room. 'This is the real world.'

'I'll be Professor Plum,' Ed was setting out the game on the table. 'Miriam you be Miss Scarlet. She's got big boobs.'

'Watch it, old son,' said Miriam. 'Or you might be playing by yourself.'

'Sorry,' grinned Ed.

They moved about the board from Dining Room to Kitchen to Conservatory.

I've got it,' shouted Ed, after about forty five minutes' play. 'It was Colonel Mustard in the Library with a rope.'

Latisha looked at the cards. It was really Mrs White in the Kitchen with the Lead Piping.

'You're absolutely right,' she lied. 'Well done, Ed. You've won the game.' She caught Miriam's puzzled expression and added, before the latter could object. 'Now you can go to bed knowing you're the champion Cluedo player in this house.'

Ed beamed and Miriam got the message. 'Well done,' she said, shuffling the cards before Ed saw the deception. 'Take an extra piece of cake for your supper. In fact, if you like, you can take your supper to bed. I'll put it on a tray for you.'

'Really?' Ed could not believe his luck. All this good fortune in one night. 'I'm glad it's you that's here and not Aunt Edie,' he said to Latisha.

'Ed!' exclaimed Miriam. 'What a rotten thing to say about

poor Aunt Edie.' Though, secretly, she was feeling guilty about feeling glad for the same reason.

When Ed had been disposed of, the two girls sat on the sagging sofa to watch the video.

'Any news of Harry?' Miriam was almost afraid to ask in case Latisha sank into a depressed silence. 'Did you see his mother?'

Latisha spread out her hands. 'Not a peep,' she said. 'But his Ma has come round to believing that, like Lou says, Harry's just doing this to give her the runaround.'

'Right,' agreed Miriam.

'Well, I don't know,' said Latisha. 'Sometimes I think she might be right. Still, it wouldn't be like Harry not to contact me. He knows I'd worry. Anyway,' she took out the video. 'I'm glad you asked me over. I'd only mope about if I stayed home. Look, this is a horror. I hope you like horrors.'

'What's it called?' asked Miriam. She would have preferred to watch MTV, but there would be time for that afterwards. After all, there was nobody to tell them when to go to bed - they could stay up until daybreak if they wanted to.

'It's one of those Freddie's Nightmare things.'

'Must be Freddie number ninety,' laughed Miriam. 'They're always churning out those loony horrors.' She was sorry she had said that; it was decent of Latisha to bring the film. 'I mean, they're popular ...'

Latisha laughed. 'They're daft, but it will give us a giggle. Turn off the light.'

After half an hour, the two girls huddled together in the flickering gloom as Freddie flashed his sabre fingernails and laughed evilly through the mist and fog of a terrified town.

The sharp tone of the telephone caused the two girls to shriek and clutch one another.

'It's only the phone,' said Miriam with relief. 'Probably Aunt Edie ringing to see if we've survived this far. I'll tell her we're working on a project on Frederick the Great. That'll keep her happy. Turn down the sound.'

30

Latisha switched on the lamp as Miriam made her way to the phone.

'Hello,' Miriam listened for a moment and looked over at Latisha. 'A reverse charge local call?' She put her hand over the mouthpiece and grinned. 'Some joker wants to make a reverse local call. Probably a broke heavy breather. That's all we need in the middle of a horror film. I'll tell the operator no thanks...'

'No, wait,' Latisha chuckled and got up. 'When he starts his heavy breathing, we'll both scream as loudly as we can and burst his eardrums. That'll teach him.'

Miriam smiled and nodded. 'All right, operator, I'll accept the call.' She and Latisha suppressed their giggles. Then a different voice came on the line.

'Lou! It's Lou.' Miriam laughed. 'We were just going to ... what?'

Her expression changed to one of concern. 'Now? Are you serious, Lou? It's half past ten ... Ring Latisha? Actually she's here with me. I'll try ... what? Okay, we'll be there.'

'What was all that about?' asked Latisha as Miriam put down the phone. 'What does Lou want?'

Miriam shook her head. 'He's at the derelict site,' she said. 'He left his art project there earlier today and went back to get it. He says ...' she paused and looked at Latisha. 'He says he's found Harry's jacket hidden in the grass. It's ... it's bloodstained.'

'Oh my God!' Latisha put her hand to her mouth. 'Oh, Miriam.'

'He's there now - at the site. He wants us to go there to meet him now. He feels Harry must be there somewhere, perhaps injured. He thinks we should have one more look for him before calling the police in case ... in case he's in some sort of trouble.'

'Well then, let's go,' said Latisha.

'What about Ed?' asked Miriam. 'I can't leave him on his own.'

'No, of course not,' agreed Latisha.

'I could ask Mrs Brown next door to keep an eye on him,

but she'd tell Mum and Dad and they'd want to know where I'd been. That would cause a monumental fuss.'

'We could bring him along,' suggested Latisha. 'Wrap him up well. Tell him it's an adventure and that he can only come if he swears not to breathe a word to anyone.'

Miriam looked doubtful. 'I suppose ...' she said. Then she brightened. 'Well, it can't do any harm. I'll go and get him.'

Ed was delighted to be part of a secret adventure with the girls. He crossed his heart that he would not tell their parents.

'If you tell, we'll never take you on an adventure like this ever again,' said Latisha. 'You're a very lucky boy to get asked like this.'

Ed beamed and crossed his heart again. He even wore his woolly hat to please Miriam.

The street was quiet when they reached the derelict site and the trio slipped under the loose plank.

'Are we playing hide and seek?' asked Ed.

'Sort of,' replied Miriam.

'Lou,' Latisha called softly. A torch flashed from one of the lower windows and came towards them.

'You were quick,' said Lou as he drew up beside them. He stopped when he saw Ed. 'What's the kid doing here?' he asked.

'I couldn't leave him on his own, could I,' retorted Miriam. 'He'll be okay. I'll look after him. What have you found?'

Lou produced Harry's grimy, fake leather jacket and thrust it into the torchlight.

Latisha gasped. 'It's Harry's all right. I recognise that tear from the time he tried to swing from a For Sale sign on our road. Oh God, Lou, what does it mean - those bloodstains ...'

'Don't let's get alarmed yet,' put in Lou. 'We must look around thoroughly. He might be injured somewhere.'

The thoughts of going into those derelict buildings again, but this time in the dark, filled Miriam with dread.

Six

Keeping a tight grip on Ed's hand, Miriam followed the other two as Lou led them to the spot where he had found Harry's jacket. She wished she had the courage to tell them that this was a total waste of time, that Harry was probably miles from here by now. Unless ... she swallowed hard ... unless he was dead. In which case they might find his body and that would freak her out altogether. She wished that none of this was happening, that she and Latisha were cosily watching stupid Freddie and that Ed was safe in bed.

'Harry,' Latisha was calling softly. 'Harry, it's us.' She lowered her voice and spoke to Lou and Miriam. 'It's important that he knows it's us,' she explained. 'Harry has a horror of people in authority. If he thought we were police or health care workers or something he'd stay holed up.'

'Why?' asked Lou. 'Has he something to hide?'

'He had a hard time as a kid,' went on Latisha. 'His old man did a runner and his Ma ... well, she wasn't going to let a kid put in on her career. She works as a singer in a nightclub - a sleazy sort of joint but it pays fairly well. Anyway, Harry's Granny lived with them and she looked after Harry. Then she died and he was left alone nights. He didn't mind, he was ten by then and able to look after himself. His Ma would get up around noon and have a hot meal ready for him when he came in from school.'

'So, what happened?' asked Miriam. 'There are worse situations in lots of homes.'

'Some busybody reported Harry's Ma. Said she was neglecting her child and all that stuff. The authorities moved in and Harry was taken into care. He was devastated. His old lady wasn't exactly Mother Goose, but she was all he had and he loved her. Of course she went ballistic and only made things worse. Screaming matches with the health care people didn't help. Harry ran away several times to try and get home, but they always caught him. Then he was put in a number of foster homes. Never settled anywhere.' Latisha paused.

'So?' prompted Lou, grunting as he pulled a plank out of the way.

'So, finally they brought him back, after a year or so. No one could manage him. His Ma was warned that she'd have to undertake to look after him properly or he would be put in a place he'd never escape from and she'd never see him again. She gave up her singing and took a day job as waitress in a trucker caff.'

'I thought you said she still works as a singer,' put in Miriam.

Latisha laughed. 'She does. Once the authorities saw that everything seemed okay, they left her alone. They're snowed under with work and they're understaffed because of cutbacks. Harry's Ma soon tired of the day job. She chucked it in and went back to her old haunt. Sings three nights a week and works as a croupier on the others.'

'A what?' asked Miriam.

'Croupier,' explained Lou. 'It means she deals cards, takes bets at gaming tables and stuff. She sounds like a hard old biddy.'

'Not really,' said Latisha. 'Like I said, she's not Mother Goose, but they muddle along okay together. But that's why Harry has a dread of authority - he thinks he's going to be pulled again and he couldn't go through all that. Not again.'

Miriam's curiosity got the better of her. She had to ask. 'Latisha,' she said. 'How come you're so ... so involved with Harry? All he wants to do is get out of school as soon as possible and hit the street life. You say you have huge ambitions. It doesn't fit.'

Latisha turned towards Miriam in the dark ruin. 'What doesn't fit?'

'Miriam thinks you've latched onto a loser,' said Lou.

Latisha snorted. 'Harry's no loser. If he stops hanging around casino joints and gets to stay in school for another while he'll be fine. Anyway, Harry and I go back to when we were kids. We just happen to like one another a lot.

Does that answer your question?'

Miriam shrugged in the dark. The fact that they really liked one another hadn't occurred to her. She felt guilty for her superficial thoughts. Poor Harry. No wonder Latisha was so concerned.

'We'll find him, Latisha,' she said by way of making amends in her own mind. 'We'll keep searching until we do.'

'Here's where I found the jacket,' Lou was shining the light into a high wilderness of weeds. 'I didn't disturb anything in case ...' he left the sentence unfinished, but the girls knew he meant in case it was murder and the police had to be called. Latisha gave a shiver and Miriam wanted to reach out and touch her. Instead she squeezed Ed's hand.

'Those weeds look pretty disturbed already,' said Latisha.

'Yes,' agreed Lou. 'It looks like there was a bit of a struggle ...'

'Bit of a struggle!' exclaimed Ed. 'It looks like millions of elephants jumped all over it.'

'Shine the light around, Lou,' said Latisha. 'If we look carefully we might find something else.'

They felt around in the damp grass for anything that might relate to Harry. They knew it was really rather pointless, but they each felt they had to be doing something. Miriam licked a finger that had been stung by a nettle and wished one of the others would call this search off. Well, she certainly wouldn't be the one, and she began to feel around the grass again. Even if they knew what they were looking for ...

'What's this?' A cry went up from Ed. Lou shone the torch in the direction of Ed who was almost concealed behind a clump of tall grass. Trust Ed to treat all this as a big adventure, thought Miriam.

'What have you found, Ed?' asked Lou.

'I don't know. Come on up here and shine the light.'

The others made their way through the thick undergrowth to where Ed was standing triumphantly in front of what appeared to be a large, circular metal thing.

'Ed, it's only a manhole cover,' said Miriam. 'You daft kid ...'

'No, wait!' exclaimed Lou. 'Look, this manhole cover is shiny at the edges.'

'So what?' said Miriam, feeling slightly ashamed that her kid brother had got them excited over nothing. No need for Lou to humour the child.

'I know what you mean,' put in Latisha. 'This place has been buried under weeds and grass for years and years. Yet that cover looks like it's been in use many times.'

Realisation dawned on Miriam. Once again she'd got it wrong.

'Good for you, Ed,' she said with forced good-will.

'Let's see if we can move it,' said Lou.

The four of them gripped the cover under the rim and heaved. It was very heavy, but eventually they could feel it moving.

'Nearly there,' grunted Lou. 'Just another heeeeaaave.'

With a thud the manhole cover fell back on the grass. The four youngsters peered into the deep pit as Lou shone his torch down. There was a damp, fetid smell from the yawning black hole. The light did not reach the bottom. There were metal steps leading downward. Lou shone the light on them.

'Look at that!' he said excitedy. 'Those steps are shiny too. They've been in constant use as well. This is weird stuff.'

Miriam drew back and rested her hand on the grass.

'Ouch,' she said as something sharp bit into her finger.

'What's wrong?' asked Lou, shining the light on her.

'Take that out of my face, Lou,' she said. 'I just pricked my finger on something sharp. It's nothing.'

But thorough Lou shone the light around Miriam to find the cause of her pricked finger. She wished he wouldn't make a fuss.

'What's that?' He focused the light on Miriam's knee. Latisha leaned closer, picked up something and gasped.

'It's Harry's earring,' she whispered. 'It's his Maltese

cross earring. He always puts it on as soon as he comes in from school. Oh, God. What does this mean? Do you think,' she tried to keep the hysteria out of her voice. 'Do you think Harry's down there?'

Her question met with a shocked quiet.

'We'd better get to the police,' Miriam whispered eventually. 'This is way out of our ...'

'No!' exclaimed Latisha. 'No,' she repeated more softly. 'Harry could be lying down there badly injured. He could be dead by the time we get help.' She took a deep breath. 'I'm going down there. Lou, may I have your torch?'

Lou waved the torch. 'I'm coming with you,' he said.

'Me too,' put in Ed.

Miriam nodded in the dark. 'Okay,' she said. 'I'll come too.'

For a moment the moon peered out from behind the night clouds as the four children lowered themselves into the black opening in the ground behind the tall, whispering weeds.

Seven

'I'll lead,' whispered Lou. 'I have the torch. I'll flash it ahead to see where we're going and then turn it off. So long as we've seen the terrain we'll be able to manage in the dark. Then I'll turn it on again to see the next few yards. We must hold on to each other.'

He shone the torch down the tunnel. The dark beyond the glow seemed evil and endless. Miriam clutched Latisha's hand and Latisha responded by giving hers a reassuring squeeze.

'Now,' said Lou. 'I'm going to turn the light off now.'

The sudden darkness enveloped them.

'Why not just leave the torch on?' asked Miriam with a touch of impatience..

'I figure we're going to be depending on the torch.' Lou's voice sounded distant and disembodied.'We'll just have to spare the batteries. I don't know how long these ones are in. It's my brother's torch.'

'I think we had better move as quietly as possible,' whispered Latisha. 'We don't know what scumbag punks might be down here with Harry.'

That sobering thought sent a prickly feeling down the back of Miriam's neck.

'Don't worry,' she whispered in Ed's ear. 'I'll look after you.'

'Worry?' exclaimed Ed.

'Sssshhh.'

'What do you mean worry?' He lowered his voice to a loud whisper. 'I'm not worried. This is neat.'

They fell into a pattern of shuffling quietly in the dark, stopping to listen before Lou turned on the torch and then progressing again.

They seemed to have been walking for hours. Miriam felt her legs ache and she knew from Ed's gait that he was exhausted, but the little beggar would never admit it - not on what he thought was a cool adventure. She wanted to ask for a rest, but Latisha would want to press on to find her Harry. And rightly so. That was the most important thing - to find Harry. Think positive.

Lou switched on the torch again. There was a curve in the tunnel. He kept the light on until they had rounded the corner.

'Oh shoot!' said Lou, focusing the light along the new ground. 'It's just more of same.'

Latisha sighed. 'Maybe we ought to turn back ...'

'Hold on,' said Lou. 'We've come this far, we might as well go another few yards. This tunnel has to lead somewhere.'

'What is it?' asked Ed.

'What's what?' Lou turned out the light again.

'This here tunnel. What do you think it is, Lou?'

'I'd say it's a very old sewer,' whispered Lou. 'Judging by the brickwork, that's what I'd say it is.'

'Yecchhh,' said Ed.

'Sssshhh,' said Latisha.

Miriam turned her head around to relieve the tense stiffness in her neck.

'What's that?' she hissed.

'What?' The others stopped.

'Behind us. Sort of sparky lights.'

Sure enough, just at the bend, there was a little spit of minute sparks which would have been invisible in the torchlight.

'Stay there,' Lou ordered. He went back the short distance and shone the torch into the niche from which the sparks were flickering.

'Bloody hell!' he exclaimed. He ran towards the other three and pushed them roughly ahead of him. 'It's explosives! Run!' He kept the torch switched on and the light danced crazily on the tunnel walls as the foursome ran, with adrenalin pumping from full-blown panic.

'Move!' urged Lou.

Afterwards none of them could quite recall what happened next. One moment they were running, the next they were sprawled in clouds of dust that gushed up from behind and caused them to gag and cough. There was a deafening, terrifying rumble as though the whole tunnel was about to collapse.

Latisha was the first to move. 'Is everyone all right?' she spluttered, brushing bits of debris off her hair. Lou had lost the torch, but luckily it was still shining where it had landed. He reached out and retrieved it, flashing it around to check on the others. Miriam was rubbing her leg where a piece of stone had cut a small gash.

'Ed,' she called out. 'Ed!' There was panic in her voice.

'I'm okay,' a muffled sound came from under a heap of rubble. Lou ran and helped the child up. Ed's grimy face beamed out from the film of grey dust. Miriam let out a sigh of relief.

'You're one cool kid, Ed,' Lou said as he brushed him down. 'Other eight-year-olds would be yelling, but not you. You're something else.'

Ed puffed out his chest proudly. Miriam could see that he was near to tears, but Lou's words made him hold them back.

'Jeez, Lou,' said Latisha. 'If you hadn't recognised those explosives we'd be ... we'd be ...'

'History,' finished Lou. 'Lucky Miriam spotted them.' He shone the torch towards Miriam. 'You okay?' he asked.

Miriam was shaking as shock began to overcome her. She felt the blood drain from the back of her head and her whole body trembled uncontrollably. She tried to speak, but her teeth were clenched. Dammit, she thought. Why was it she who had to let the side down? As the others made their way across to her, a sudden powerful light shone into their faces.

'Visitors!' said a harsh, commanding voice. 'I was right. There were voices. Take them below. Use the batons if necessary.'

Lou held up his hands to shield his eyes from the light. In a flash he assessed the situation. The voices were only yards away. He grabbed Ed roughly by the arm.

'Run!' he shouted to the others. Half carrying Ed, he galloped back along the way they'd come, praying that, by some miracle, the explosion would have left even a small opening. Miriam sprinted after him, fear giving unnatural speed to her feet. The angry voices pursued them and, when their lights revealed a solid wall of rubble, they knew all was lost. As rough hands dragged Lou and the loudly protesting Ed away, Miriam cast her eyes desperately upwards to where a pinhole of night sky was visible at the top of the pile. If only she could be out there under that sky, she'd never take anything for granted ever again.

Eight

With the blinding light shining in their eyes, the four youngsters were bundled roughly along the tunnel. They could see only the dim outlines of their captors, who stayed behind the lanterns, but they could feel the angry prods of their fists.

'Who are you and where the hell do you think you're taking us?' Lou demanded in an even voice. He was answered with a thump from a stick.

Realising they were up against a particularly vicious group, the others stayed quiet. A menacing aura, both terrifying and silent emanated from these men. To fight them would be pointless.

After a short distance the tunnel became narrower. They had to walk in single file so there wasn't even the comfort of touching one another.

After a long, stumbling and suffocating trudge, the lanterns lit up a low, wooden door. It was almost concealed in the wall of the tunnel. One of the men stepped forward into the light and, grasping a heavy, iron ring, pulled it open. He was a tall, thin man with bony fingers. He wore a crumpled suit of some sort of rough material. But it was his face that made the four captives gasp. The skeletal frame of his face was covered with pasty, porridge-like flesh that stretched across the cheekbones giving him a deathly appearance. His heavy eyebrows dipped in an angry frown under which glittering eyes glared with manic intensity. He took a lantern from one of the others and preceded them through the narrow opening.

'Enter,' one of the other men pushed Miriam. She gasped as she staggered through the door. The air in this tiny passage was stifling. There wasn't room to stand straight and her elbows grazed off the stony sides. This was unreal. What was she doing here, chasing after a rough type like Harry with two people she hardly knew? Could this nightmare please finish and let her wake up to find herself

42

back in her old, familiar home or in safe, secure St Elizabeth's where she would have met none of these people and would certainly not be down in a place like this, hauling her young brother into some weird danger.

'Move,' a gruff voice urged from behind. Miriam felt a claustrophobic panic rise in her chest. I won't panic, she mouthed to herself. I won't panic. I won't panic. But, when the passageway became even narrower and she had to stoop almost double, she freaked out. She thought of the line of people behind and the rough maniac ahead - there was no way out! The scream took her over completely, all reasoning lost in a phobic panic. She turned around awkwardly. Her voice came out in a gulping staccato.

'I have to get out of here. I have to get out. Oh, please let me out!' The back of her neck was damp and her head felt strange. The man in front turned and gave her a blow across the back with his stick. In her panic Miriam didn't seem to notice. She was clinging to Latisha who was behind her, clawing at her shoulders and gasping in terror.

Lou reached over Latisha's shoulder and grasped Miriam's hand. 'It's all right, Miriam,' he was shouting to control her panic. 'Take deep breaths and hang on for a little longer. Back off, scumbag!' he yelled at the man who again laid his stick across Miriam's back. She shuddered and fell against Latisha. By now the other men were crushing against the small group around Miriam.

'Get on your feet and move, girl,' one of them shouted.

'Can't you see she's terrified?' Latisha put her arms around Miriam. 'She's got claustrophobia. Get back. Give her room.'

By now Ed's brave front broke down and he began to cry. Lou took his arm before one of the men could grab him.

'Not now, Ed,' he whispered. 'We need you, kid. Hang in there.'

Ed bit his lip and clung to Lou. The man in front had taken Miriam by the shoulder and was pulling her along the passage.

'It's all right,' Latisha was calling to her, keeping very

close behind. 'We're not going to be here for long, just think of that. These goons are taking us somewhere, but we'll be out of here.'

Sure enough they stopped at another door which the man ahead unlocked. A surge of air came through into the passage and the group automatically filled their lungs deeply. They surged out onto a wooden platform and stared in disbelief at the scene below.

'Jeez!' gasped Lou.

An enormous cavern stretched out in all directions, as far as the eye could see. Wooden houses were clustered together in small groups. Except for those in the centre, most of the houses appeared to be derelict. Lanterns, similar to the ones the men were carrying, flickered with an eerie glow over the rooftops. In the distance there appeared to be a big green patch, like a garden. Before the astonished youngsters could take in much more of this bizarre place, they were bundled down wooden steps onto the earthy surface.

'Where, Samuel?' one of the men asked. 'The meeting hall?'

The man with the skeletal face and bony fingers shook his head. 'Detention house,' he said.

The men ushered the group across the primitive street to a solidly-built wooden structure which had just one window, very high up.

'Just a second,' Latisha found her voice as the man they called Samuel inserted a big, old-fashioned key into the iron lock. 'You can't do this. You can't just lock people up and ... get your filthy paws off me!' Her tone changed as she was pushed through the door along with the others. They stared at one another with disbelief in the gloom as the door slammed and the key grated in the lock with awful finality.

'Is this for real?' whispered Latisha.

'Hey!' a voice called from a corner of the room. They swung around, startled.

'Harry?' Latisha recognised the voice first. 'Harry!'

Sure enough it was Harry who emerged from a

shadowy corner. His chest was bare and his face was bruised. There was dried blood under his nostrils.

Latisha ran to him. 'Well, at least we've found you,' she said.

Harry gave a crooked smile. 'Can't say I'm glad to to see you lot,' he said. 'Now we're all in the shit.' He looked over at Lou and Miriam, who had her arms around Ed. 'How did you ...' both he and Lou started to say together.

'You first,' said Lou.

Harry snorted, which caused another trickle of blood to come from his nose. He wiped it with the back of his hand. Miriam fished in the pocket of her jeans and silently handed him a tatty tissue. He wiped his nose again before he spoke.

'It was that medal thing,' he said. 'The silver thing I found, remember?'

Latisha nodded.

'When I got home I got to thinking that it might be valuable. I know from the feel of it that it was silver. The more I thought about it, the more I felt that it would fetch me some much needed cash. I thought to myself, "I'll show Miss Latisha. I'll find that thing and flash the cash in her face when I get paid for it."'

'Oh, Lou. You silly prat,' Latisha said softly.

'So you went back,' put in Lou.

Harry nodded. 'Took my flashlight and headed back after my Ma went out to work. I had a fair idea where Latisha had tossed it so I was sure I'd find it. I was poking around in the grass when I heard a scraping noise. I doused the light, thought it might be druggies who wouldn't take kindly to me being on their turf.' He sighed and wiped his nose again. Some of the grubby tissue stuck to the dried blood on his upper lip. 'There was just enough light for me to see this manhole cover being pushed back,' he went on. 'Two shadowy figures hopped out and I froze. I swear I didn't make a sound, but still they knew I was there. It's as if they heard me breathing. It was freaky. They came straight over, grabbed me and thumped me about. I knew I was up against a couple of pros so I tried to do a runner. One of them caught my jacket and I slipped out of it.'

'That's what we found,' said Latisha. 'That's how ...'

'Ssshhh,' said Lou. 'Go on, Harry.'

'Well there was no way they were going to let me go. I stumbled and tripped across the dark site, but those boys seemed to know every square inch. They moved like oiled shadows, headed me off and, before I knew it I was being hauled along well ... you know. You've probably just been along that route.'

There was a grunt from the darkened corner of the room. Then a rattle of chains. Harry stopped and looked in the direction of the sound. The rattling sound drew closer and a thin, ragged figure came into sight. Ed buried his face in Miriam's sweater when he saw the manacles that were chained to the man's skinny legs.

'This is Ralph,' said Harry. 'He can tell us something about these ghouls.'

Nine

Ralph stood silently looking at the newcomers for a moment. His eyes were bright and intelligent, but his appearance smacked of brutal neglect. His fair hair was matted, like an old Sindy doll. He had a straggly beard which grew in uneven wisps giving him a wild appearance. He looked very old, but in fact when you looked more closely at his face, he was quite a young man.

'Ralph's been here for about seven years,' said Harry. 'He was taken along with ...' He looked apologetically at Ralph, as if sorry he'd mentioned it - 'along with his kid brother.'

'Taken? You mean kidnapped?' queried Lou.

Ralph nodded slightly. 'Let's sit,' he said, shuffling back to the dark corner. The others followed. There were rough blankets on some torn mattresses where Ralph and Harry had obviously been resting. They sat and focused their attention on Ralph, anxious to know more about this nightmare place and its people.

'These are dangerous people,' Ralph began.

'We know that,' said Lou. 'We felt their fists. Who are they? They're like ... like the undead.'

'They are, practically,' agreed Ralph. 'They're a bunch of religious freaks gone wrong.'

'Religious?' Latisha said. 'I wouldn't have thought anything so ...'

'Ssshh. Let the man speak,' Harry said, pulling a rug around his naked shoulders. 'Listen. You won't believe this. Go on, Ralph.'

Ralph stretched out his manacled legs and leaned forward on his mattress. 'They call themselves The Dwellers,' he said. 'The Dwellers Beneath, to give them their full title. They trace back to Victorian times ... '

'Do you mean that lot out there ... ?' began Miriam.

Ralph shook his head in the shadowy gloom. 'No. They're the descendants of the original lot. They were a sect that formed during the industrial revolution back then. They believed that machinery was evil. That the factories which grew up in great numbers were taking people from rural pastures and turning them into materialistic money-grabbers, sinners beyond redemption. They thought that people were cramming into sin-filled ghettos in cities which bred hellish evil. They saw the factory chimneys take over the landscape and decided they'd seen enough, that mankind was doomed to a hell on earth.'

'So?' prompted Lou as Ralph paused to rub a weal on his ankle.

'So they decided to go underground.'

'Just like that?' Lou snapped his fingers.

'Shut up, Lou,' said Latisha, leaning towards Ralph. 'Go on, Ralph.'

'Not immediately. They searched for years until they found a cavern suitable for their needs. Then they bought the surrounding land. They had engineers and craftsmen in their group, as well as farmers and a doctor. Over the next few years, they lowered all the equipment they needed into this place. And I mean everything; they've even managed to continually breed from the original goats and chickens that were brought down all those years ago. They were completely self-sufficient.'

'Not for crops, surely,' said Latisha. 'How could they grow crops?'

'Mirrors,' said Ralph.

'Mirrors?'

'Yes. Their engineers constructed a huge complex of faceted mirrors ...' He pointed upwards. 'There's an opening right at the top of the cave where they lowered everything down in the beginning.'

'An opening?' put in Lou. 'Couldn't that be seen from above?'

Ralph shook his head. 'Those bods thought of everything. The opening is high in a barren, rocky area in the middle of the land they'd bought. No one can buy that land or develop it in any way. It's protected by deeds in the bank. Incidentally, so is that site where the other entrance is - the one that we all came down. That was a disused sewer. They bought the houses surrounding that manhole too.'

'So that's why that place has never been developed,' exclaimed Latisha. 'The deeds are all tied up too.'

'Right,' said Ralph. 'Anyway, once everything was in place, the engineers constructed the faceted mirrors ...'

'What's faceted?' asked Ed.

'Oh, for heaven's sake let Ralph go on,' said Lou impatiently.

'It means,' Ralph explained to Ed. 'It means that they had hundreds of mirrors facing in all directions which reflected the sunlight down here - at least down onto the area they'd filled with tons of soil from the land. That meant they were able to grow things. There's an underground river at the far end of the settlement which supplies their water and irrigates the land.'

'They thought of everything,' said Lou with a certain amount of awe.

'Yes,' agreed Ralph. 'It certainly seemed like that. They even managed to plumb into the town gas pipes without ever being detected.'

'But they must have needed stuff,' said Latisha. 'Surely they ran out of raw materials, medicines ...?'

'I was coming to that,' agreed Ralph. 'When they discovered that they would need certain things, as you mentioned, they trained men called Scouts to go above and steal whatever was needed. Only basic things, mind you; paraffin, medicines - as you said, cloth, things like that. And only things that didn't smack of the twentieth century. Nothing modern was allowed down.'

'Nothing at all?' exclaimed Miriam.

'Well just one bit. I'll come to that.'

'What,' put in Ed. 'What modern thing?'

'Shush Ed,' said Latisha. 'Go on, Ralph. I can't believe all this stuff.'

Ralph nodded. 'Those fellows were well trained,' he said. 'They moved like shadows and never got caught. Scouts wore special silver medallions which marked them off as special Dwellers. Those medallions had a religious verse written on them to protect the Scouts from the evils

Above.'

'See? It was silver,' put in Harry.

'Everything went well for the first forty years or so,' went on Ralph. 'Then things began to go wrong. Lack of ... I don't know ... vitamins, proper air, who knows? Anyway more and more babies were born either dead or else very weak. The sect thought it was some punishment from God and they started getting stricter and stricter in their religious activities. More rules, more prayers until life was just one long guilt trip. Still their babies died and then people began to get illnesses which didn't get better. Death claimed not just babies and the elderly, but young people as well. Their numbers began to decline rapidly. They realised that something drastic had to be done or the sect would die out.'

Miriam wanted to ask him how he knew all of this, but she would draw the wrath of the others if she interrupted, so she kept silent.

'That's when they started kidnapping babies,' Ralph looked up at the spellbound faces. 'The Scouts were told to abduct babies; healthy looking babies. They were to compensate for the ones they lost. You're all probably too young to remember the panic about ten years ago when there was a mysterious spate of baby kidnappings. There were all sorts of theories, from aliens to satanic cults. But the mystery was never solved.'

'I remember my mother mentioning that,' said Latisha. 'There are more kidnappings now, but it's older kids ...'

'That's it,' said Harry. 'It's this shower who are doing it!'

'You mean, all those kids who've disappeared recently - they're down here?' Latisha looked at Ralph, wide-eyed. He was nodding.

'But why,' put in Lou, 'didn't they take enough kids then? Why go through all that again?'

'Because those babies died.' There was a shocked pause.

'You mean all of them?' asked Miriam softly. 'They all just died.'

Ralph was shaking his head sadly. 'Every one of them.' He cleared his throat. 'Including my own kid brother.

None of them survived beyond the age of seven or eight. This place just killed them.'

'Jeez!' swore Lou.

'That's how I come to be here,' continued Ralph. 'I was babysitting on the night they took our Jamie. I was watching telly. Jamie was in his pram beside me. I didn't bother to draw the curtains ...' He stopped to clear his throat again. 'I heard a noise in the kitchen. "Bloody cats," I said and went to investigate. One of those shadowy buggers faced me in the kitchen. The other dashed in and grabbed Jamie. They must have been watching the house. Must have seen my folks go out - that's the way they operate - patient watching and waiting until they're sure of their ... their prey. Anyway I tried to fight them off, but I was only twelve at the time. I kept running after them and shouting until they came to the place we called the Haunted Site - the place that you found too. Well, I saw one of them go down the manhole, he was the one who was carrying Jamie. I raced after him, but the other one was lying in wait for me. He jumped me and knocked me out. And ... well, I'm here ever since.' He paused and fiddled with a link on his chain.

Lou pursed his lips, as if he wanted to say something but didn't know which words to use. He cleared his throat.

'Tell me,' he began. 'Why have they let you ... you know?'

'Stay alive, you mean?' said Ralph.

Lou nodded. 'Yeah. Why didn't they just kill you?'

Ralph gave a bitter laugh. 'Lucky for me I was a bit of a swot as a kid. I was big into electronics and stuff like that. At school we had just done magnetism and electricity with old Mad Jones - is he still there?' He looked up at Lou.

Lou shrugged and looked at the others. They shrugged too.

'Probably retired,' said Ralph. 'He was old back then.'

'Go on about the electricity,' prompted Latisha.

'Yes,' went on Ralph, 'well, I had a fair idea how to make a basic generator from water power - that river has a pretty strong flow. While they were deciding what to do with me

I was looking around for anything that would help me survive. I could see that they were having a problem with food and medicines going off.'

'So you told them you could fix that,' put in Lou.

Ralph nodded. 'I knew that if I was to live it would only be because I had something to offer. So I told them I could power a fridge.'

'And they believed you,' said Miriam. 'Were you really able to do it?'

Ralph grinned. 'I was always a bit of a chancer. But I made bloody sure I could do it. We rigged up a makeshift fridge but it does the job. Has been doing it all these years.'

'And that's the modern thing,' said Ed, 'the one you said was the only modern thing they have.'

'That's right, kid,' smiled Ralph. 'And I make sure that I'm the only one who knows the full workings of that fridge. It's my survival pack. It's why they've kept me alive all this time.'

There was silence while the others took this on board.

Then Lou spoke softly. 'We have no skills,' he said.

'Does that mean they are going to kill us?' Ed's high-pitched, childish voice rang out. Miriam reached out and held him to her, as if to shut out the awful thought. She glared at Lou who bit his lip and looked apologetic.

'Ralph,' Latisha broke in, 'why are they now taking older children? It doesn't make sense.'

'Because they are more robust than babies,' replied Ralph. 'They're past the infant stage. They have a better chance of survival down here. All they have to do is brainwash these kids and the stupid sect is saved. New blood to carry on the cult.'

'It ... it's totally unreal,' whispered Miriam.

'There it is,' said Ralph with a shrug. 'No point in sparing your feelings. I have to tell it like it is.'

'Maybe with so many of us here now we can work something out,' said Harry, hopefully. 'Maybe we could break out and head back along the tunnel. We'd know the way.'

Ralph hung his head. 'Not any more,' his voice sounded

dismal. He looked up at Harry. 'Remember that loud rumble we heard earlier?'

Harry nodded.

'That was an explosion in the tunnel,' went on Ralph. 'Am I right?' He turned to Lou.

'Yes,' said Lou, 'it only just missed us.'

'The whole tunnel just blew up,' Ed added. 'Poff! Just like that.'

'That's their seal,' explained Ralph.

'Seal,' asked Latisha.

'Yes,' Ralph continued. 'They planted those explosives there years ago. If ever anyone discovered the entrance from the town side, the plan was to blow up that part of the tunnel, thus sealing off this end. Obviously when Harry here found the entrance they decided to use that seal.'

'And to think it just missed us,' said Miriam. 'Seconds later and we'd be ...' she clutched her brother.

'How do you know so much?' asked Lou, voicing Miriam's question.

'I listen,' said Ralph. 'By listening and piecing together bits of conversation, I got the picture after a while. They're so used to me as a lackey that they frequently talk freely while I'm about some menial task. I keep my head down and I'd advise you to do the same. I fought like a tiger when they pushed me about at first, but,' he shrugged, 'it only got me bruises and black eyes. Not worth it, believe me.'

'Brutes!' Harry gritted his teeth. 'We've got to get out of this place.'

Ten

The group huddled together on the flimsy, smelly mattresses, each one slipping in and out of a headachy doze during the next few hours, each too afraid and too bewildered to talk any more about their fears. Except for Ed; he slept soundly, his head on Miriam's lap and her arm protectively around him.

They all looked with nervous anticipation at the door when they heard the key turning in the lock. Six shadowy figures loomed against the dim glow that came from outside. Now that they were in a position to better see their captors, their hearts sank. Like Samuel, the other men had skeletal features and complexions like raw dough. Some had sores on their faces which gave them an air of decay. Miriam reached behind and squeezed Latisha's hand.

'Zombies,' Latisha whispered in her ear.

'Quiet girl,' one of the men growled. 'You'll only speak when spoken to.'

Latisha raised her eyebrows in surprise. How could he possibly have heard her low whisper at that distance?

'Up! Up!' The other men began to prod the youngsters with sticks. 'Move quickly.'

They were led out into the street. The dull glow was coming from high over their heads. Harry glanced up and saw the complex of mirrors which were indeed reflecting the rays of the sun outside. Before he could take in any more, he was pushed from behind.

'Move, boy!'

'Back off!' he retorted angrily. 'I'm moving. What more do you want?'

With a roar, another of the men lashed out with his stick, catching Harry on the arm. He winced and clutched the injured part.

'Brutes!' shouted Latisha. 'Lunatic brutes ...'

Harry grabbed her arm. 'Cool it, Latisha,' he whispered. 'Best not provoke them. They're crazy.'

'I'll show you crazy, boy!' The same man lashed out

54

again at Harry, knocking his breath out with a painful gasp. Again Latisha marvelled at the man's acute hearing. She grimaced and moved closer to Harry.

The group stopped before a long, wooden building in the middle of the street and the youngsters were urged through the thick, iron-hinged door. The inside was laid out like a simple meeting hall or chapel. The walls were painted in stark grey, unrelieved by any form of ornament. Pews which once accommodated many Dwellers, now contained a scattering of a curious few. Heads turned to scrutinise the newcomers. Ed clutched Lou's arm and hid his face from the scrutiny. There were about thirty Dwellers. Most of them were frail and middle-aged. All of them had the same doughy complexion. The few women were dressed in bonnets and long, drab dresses. They looked disapprovingly at the girls' casual clothes. With a touch of defiance, Latisha loudly clumped her Doc Martens as she walked up the worn, wooden aisle.

'Dusty old crows,' whispered Miriam.

One of the women stood up. 'Calling us names will serve you no purpose, girl,' she said grimly.

'How could she hear ...?' began Miriam in amazement.

'Quiet!' This came from the man they called Samuel. He was seated at a dais at the top of the room. He stood and clutched the sides of the dais with his bony fingers. Then he raised one hand and pointed at the group. 'You are intruders,' his deep voice belied his frail stature. 'You have come here with evil intent.'

'We have not!' Latisha's voice rang out. 'We were simply looking for Harry - who your goons kidnapped, the same as you've kidnapped those other ...'

Miriam bit her lip as a stick flew and thwacked Latisha into silence. With a sinking heart she realised that they stood no chance against these crazy people. As if to voice her despair Samuel continued.

'You will never return Above,' he said, in his funereal voice. 'You must stay here, be part of our community. You will work and serve us. And if,' his voice changed to a wheedle, 'if you prove yourselves worthy you may eventually join us.'

'Never!' spat Harry. He braced himself for another thump, but none came.

'Then you will work,' Samuel raised his voice. 'You will work or die.'

'I'd sooner ...,' began Harry, but Lou nudged him into silence.

'The manacles,' Samuel turned to the men who had brought the youngsters here. 'Take the small one to the schoolhouse.'

Miriam paled when she realised that he meant Ed. She held him to her and fought off the hands that reached for him. Ed cried out and clung to his sister. Miriam looked pleadingly at Samuel.

'Leave him with me,' she was almost sobbing in desperation. 'Please. He's only a little boy ...'

'Precisely,' said Samuel. 'The small ones are our salvation.'

Ed was dragged screaming from the meeting hall. Miriam tried to go after him, but she was forced into a seat with the others. Latisha gripped her hand sympathetically. She could find no words of comfort to give the distraught girl. The boys struggled as the manacles were being put on, but it was useless.

Afterwards they were led out again. The two boys were pushed towards the green area at the far end of the cave. Two of the women took charge of Latisha and Miriam, leading them to a long building near the meeting hall. Inside it was lined with worn and chipped sinks. A cast iron range stood at one end with big pots simmering on top. Lines stretched across the ceiling.

'The laundry,' whispered Latisha.

'Yes,' said one of the women. 'You will work here to help our worthy endeavour.'

'Wash by hand?' Latisha feigned helplessness. 'I've never washed by hand in my life.'

The woman put her pasty face close to Latisha's. 'Insolence will serve only pain and deprivation, girl. You work, you eat. You don't work, you don't eat. You speak out of turn, you don't eat. You sin by attitude, you don't eat. You cause anger in the heart of our Elder, you don't eat ...'

'All right,' muttered Latisha. 'I get the message. What are we supposed to do here?'

One of the other women brought over a sack containing a bundle of discoloured clothing.

'Wash,' she said simply. Then she took a long chain and attached it to the manacles on the girls' legs, restricting their movements to the area around the sinks and the range. She handed each of them a bar of greasy soap with bits of grit embedded in them. 'When you have completed the washing, you will be given food,' she said. She gazed with open hostility at the two girls as she spoke. Her face was yellow in patches and a weeping sore beside her left nostril increased the ghoulishness of her appearance.

'Come, Sarah,' said the other. 'We must not remain in the company of sinners.'

Miriam and Latisha looked at one another as the door closed behind the two women and a bolt was fastened outside.

'Well, that's some blessing,' sighed Latisha. 'At least they won't be hanging about, breathing down our necks ... hey, Miriam. Don't go under.'

Miriam was blinking as she tried to hold back her tears. She shook her head. 'Can't help it. Sorry.'

'Oh, Miriam. Is it Ed?'

Miriam nodded. Latisha put her hands on Miriam's shoulders. 'Listen, kid,' she said. 'They're not going to harm Ed. You heard what old thunderguts said - he said that the young ones are the salvation of this cruddy lot. They're not going to harm their own salvation. Ed will be treated like ... like, well, like a saviour. They need him and the other kids. Whatever about you and me and the blokes, Ed will be okay. Got that?'

Miriam nodded again. Her nose was running and Latisha offered her a shirt from the laundry sack. 'Here,' she said. 'Wipe your snot on this and pretend its owner is still inside it.'

It was hot and steamy inside the laundry. After a few hours the girls felt they could not go on.

'Keep talking, Latisha,' said Miriam as she hoisted the pulley to raise another line of washed clothes. 'If we stop talking we'll sink into depression.'

'You're right,' sighed Latisha, wiping her forehead with the back of her wrist. 'Look at my flamin' hands.' She held them out. 'These blisters will be agony later on. And this lot think that machines are sinful? It's far more sinful to abuse the skin that the good Lord gave us. Try telling that to old Mr Megadeth. Oops! clamp the lips, here come the zombies.'

The bolt was drawn and the two women returned. This time they were accompanied by Samuel. The three of them stood and looked at the lines of washing. Latisha was about to whisper to Miriam that she hoped they wouldn't peer too closely at the clothes, but a sixth sense made her keep her mouth shut.

Samuel walked towards them. He was wearing a flat hat with a wide brim which emphasised the shadows under his eyes. On his belt a ring of keys jangled as he walked. He said nothing, but watched Miriam as she finished hoisting the last line of washing. Miriam felt uneasy under his gaze. She looked away in confusion, but, when she looked at him again, he was still staring at her. 'How old are you, girl?' he asked.

Miriam continued tying the rope that held up the line. One of the women rushed over and slapped her arm. 'Answer when Elder Samuel addresses you,' she said.

Miriam looked back at the man. He was still staring, his manic eyes glittering under the hat brim. If she answered he might shift his gaze.

'I'm ... I'm fourteen,' she muttered.

Nobody spoke and Elder Samuel turned and left, followed by the two women.

'What on earth was that about?' asked Latisha when they were alone again. 'Maybe he's planning a birthday do for you.'

Miriam appreciated Latisha's lighthearted attempt at

glossing over the incident, but deep down an even greater dread began to take hold of her.

Eleven

That evening the four exhausted friends and Ralph were returned to the detention house. Their manacles rattled as they threw themselves on the mattresses.

'What were you girls doing?' asked Harry.

'Washing,' said Latisha, stretching out her blistered hands. 'And you?'

'Harvesting potatoes,' said Harry. 'Back breaking stuff.' He arched his back as he spoke. 'They didn't even give us a cup of water.'

'Us neither,' said Latisha. 'Weren't they quick to make skivvies of us? We're only here a matter of hours and already we've done slave labour.'

'They need all the labour they can get,' said Ralph. 'Some of them are too feeble to be of much use. It's their lungs. It's always the lungs.'

Latisha looked at Miriam. 'You're not still worried about Ed, are you Miriam?'

Miriam smiled slightly. 'No. I suppose you're right. He'll be okay.'

'He will,' put in Ralph. 'I knew when I saw him that they'd take him to the other children. They're so anxious to win them over that they treat them all right. He'll go to school and get a lot of old codswallop thrown at him. Cold and extremely strict, but they won't harm him. Not physically.'

Lou was looking at Ralph with a puzzled expression. Ralph returned his gaze. 'What are you staring at?' he asked.

'I'm wondering,' said Lou.

'Wondering?'

'Yes. You surprise me. You've been here since you were twelve years old, yet you talk like an adult - in fact you talk like an old-fashioned adult. Like one of them,' he added, almost accusingly. 'And, something else, how did you manage to keep sane all this time? I've had one day here and I feel I could freak out right now. How have you managed?'

Ralph fished in the pocket of his ragged pants and drew out a key ring with a miniature Rubik's cube at the end of it. 'This,' he said. 'This kept me sane in the beginning. I know every permutation possible on this thing. This was the key of my locker at school. It was in my pocket the night I ...' he broke off and rummaged under the mattress, drawing out a bundle of very tattered pages. 'Then, when they didn't watch me so closely after a while,' he continued, 'I managed to take pages, and sometimes whole books. The original settlers took down libraries of books on a whole range of subjects. Poetry, science, agriculture, boring old essays by famous Victorian writers. At least they would have been boring to me as a kid, but I came to treasure every word I could read. I read and re-read - names like G K Chesterton, Maria Edgeworth, Dickens of course - they were like lights inside my head. I recited to myself writings that I'd learned by heart. And always - always I convinced myself that the day would come when I'd be out of here. I resolved to keep myself sane for that day.'

'All those years ...?' began Harry.

'Yes, I know. There were times when I almost went under, but I'd work myself up again. Read, recite, anything to keep my mind going. I remembered seeing a repeat of an old film when I was about seven; it was about a man who was kept in solitary confinement. They wouldn't let him read or anything. One evening, looking at the ceiling, he saw the shadow of the crossed bars of his window. He knew a little bit about chess, so he used to play imaginary games of chess each evening when the sun cast those shadows on the ceiling. That kept him sane. If there's something you can latch your mind on to, you'll get by. With me it was words. If I ever get out of this place I'll be a world authority on Victorian times. Anyway,' he thrust his books under his mattress, 'that's how I kept my sanity. I was always a boring self-sufficient kid,' he added with a grin.

Lou nodded. 'You did well,' he said with admiration.

'You're incredible. Did you ever wonder what was going on at home?'

Ralph put out his hand to stop Lou from going any further. 'No!' he said sharply. 'I don't want to know. I deliberately kept my mind off the life I'd been leading. I forced myself not to think of my family and home. I knew if I did that I'd sink. No, don't talk to me of home. I survive from day to day.'

'But there must have been times when you thought of giving in,' said Miriam. 'All that time alone.'

'I wasn't actually alone,' said Ralph. 'I was out there working among those people. They didn't talk much to me, but at least I was among them, listening to them. Some of them are fairly okay.'

'Could have fooled me,' muttered Harry. 'Bloody lunatics.'

'No, they're not lunatics,' went on Ralph. 'Far from it. But they're so - so mulishly convinced that they're right. You couldn't argue with them. They just can't listen to reason.'

'You've tried?' asked Latisha.

Ralph nodded. 'Brick wall. They want to know nothing, only their small, crumbling world down here.'

'But you must have thought of giving in,' Miriam said again. 'Were you not tempted to fall in with them so that,' she indicated the manacles, 'at least you'd have been more comfortable?'

'Oh yes,' said Ralph. He paused and looked at his dirty, calloused hands. 'But when I saw them bury my brother, I resloved that nothing they ever did would ever make me turn to their ways. We've had an uneasy stalemate ever since - I do what I do and they leave me alone.'

'I still say they're a bunch of lunatics,' Harry said. 'Porridge-faced prats. I'd like to punch them in their mangy mouths ...'

'Cool it, Harry,' said Latisha. 'This won't be solved by punches, you big twit. Try using the brain.'

Harry looked at her and grinned. He shook his chains. 'The brains in chains ... hey!' he exclaimed. 'These chains!' He was looking closely at the lock on the manacles around his legs.

'What,' asked Lou. 'What about them?'

'Only that they have simple locks,' went on Harry. 'if I had a bit of wire or something ...'

'Ssshhh,' Ralph put his hand over Harry's mouth and put his finger to his own lips. He nodded towards the door. There were voices outside and the lock was turned.

Two men carried in trays with wooden bowls on them. Two others kept guard. Without speaking, the men put down the trays and left. One of them looked curiously back at Miriam before closing the door. She shivered under his glance and reached out for a bowl.

'What have we here?' asked Lou, sniffing at the contents of his bowl. 'It smells like ... like ...'

'Like damp clothes,' said Harry. 'It smells like sports gear that's been left in a plastic bag for a week.'

'Just like yours, Harry,' laughed Latisha.

'Do you know that bit in the bible where Cain and Abel fight over a mess of potage?' said Lou.

'No,' said Latisha.

'Well,' continued Lou. 'I've often wondered what a mess of potage was. Now I know.'

'Actually it's not so bad if you hold your nose,' said Ralph. 'You'll get used to it. Eat it anyway, you'll need your strength.'

They spooned the messy stuff into their famished stomachs and felt better for the nourishment.

'Tell me something, Ralph,' Latisha said as they stacked their empty bowls on the tray. 'How come these Dweller nuts are able to hear even the merest whisper?'

'Hah, you've noticed,' said Ralph. 'Yes, they have abnormally sharp ears. It evolved through the years. I suppose living in such a silent place for so long has given them acute hearing. It made me a bit paranoid in the beginning. I used to think they could read my mind. Just be careful what you say, that's all. Don't whisper secrets if there are any of them around.'

'We've got to get out of here,' Harry stretched and went over to the window. 'Jeez, we've got to act. For heaven's sake Ralph. You've been here long enough. There must be a way.'

Ralph shrugged his shoulders. 'There are only two entrances,' he said. 'One is where the mirrors are - that's the opening where they lowered everything down in the beginning. But that's a sheer climb. It would be like trying to climb up a smooth glacier. And the other entrance, well ...' he shrugged again. 'Well, that's been sealed off with the explosion.'

Harry banged his fist on the mattress, raising a cloud of dust in the gloom.

'Except,' Ralph began doubtfully.

'Except?' Lou leaned towards him. 'Except what?'

'It's only a chance in a million,' said Ralph. 'But they get their gas from the town supply. Remember I told you that?' The others nodded.

'Well, whenever anything goes wrong with the gas supply, a couple of the men go through an opening down beyond the green area. They stay away for ages so I imagine that they have to go a long way. All the gas pipes go into that tunnel so ...'

'So?' Lou lowered his voice.

'So, if someone were to follow those pipes ...'

'I get it,' said Harry. 'Follow the pipes and come out wherever the gas tanks are stored.'

Ralph nodded. 'It's only a hunch,' he said. 'I don't know how far those pipes go, or even if they lead anywhere that a body could follow ... I'd say any opening would be pretty small, otherwise they'd risk being discovered by gas company workers. Like I said, it's just a hunch.'

'A hunch is good enough,' said Lou.

'Don't do anything rash,' added Ralph. 'Wait until tomorrow. We'll probably be picking potatoes again. The entrance is near there. Try to keep near me. I'll signal when we're in sight of the entrance. We can make plans once you've seen it. Only don't, *don't*,' he repeated, 'speak of any plans if any of these people are within a hundred yards. Don't even look pleased.'

Harry was standing on his toes, peering out. 'They're

drawing down the mirrors,' he said as a distant clanking sound reached them.

'That's the evening ritual,' said Ralph. 'When the sun goes down, they fold up the mirrors. In a few minutes you'll hear chanting. That'll be the nightly praying. Elder Samuel delivers a fire and brimstone sermon and they all go to their beds with their nightly fix of guilt to lull them to sleep.'

'And the children?' asked Miriam. 'Do the children have to sit through that too?'

Ralph nodded. 'We can only hope that they let it run off them,' he said softly.

Miriam tried to imagine Ed, who was a child of the nineties, fond of computer games and sci-fi like Power Rangers, listening to Elder Samuel's droning. She just hoped he'd dismiss it as hocus pocus. She wished she could see him, comfort him and reassure him that they'd all get out somehow. She sighed. She would never growl at him again. Not ever. But how would they ever get out? Her mind raged with the wish that they could kill those evil Dwellers and get back to the air and normality of life above these caves.

'What I was saying,' Harry said in a low voice, 'is that, with a bit of wire I know I could open these here handcuffs - legcuffs- whatever they're called.'

'You could?' Ralph leaned closer to him.

'Yeah I learnt that stuff in ... in a place I was in. They're simple locks. No problem.'

'No,' Lou turned from the window and came back to sit on the mattress.

'What do you mean "no"?' Harry looked at him.

'Not yet, Harry,' said Lou. 'If you open them now, they'll just put stronger ones on, or split us up or something. No. Better to wait until we case the place and see what plans we can come up with.' He took off his glasses to wipe them on his sweatshirt. Circles of grime surrounded his eyes where the glasses had been. Miriam felt she wanted to hug him for his quiet, confident and practical ideas. If anyone could guide them through this it would be clever Lou.

'He's right,' agreed Ralph. 'It's tempting to do it, but it would be better to wait until we can make more definite plans.'

Miriam felt heartened at the talk of escape. She glanced at Latisha who nodded encouragingly back.

Twelve

In the morning Miriam was stiff all over and had only
dozed fitfully. She eased her arm from under Latisha's
head and rubbed it to get the circulation going again.
Latisha stirred and opened her eyes. She looked at Miriam
for a moment before realising that she had not been having
a bad dream. This was real. Before she could say anything,
there was a loud clanking and clattering from outside. The
two girls raised their heads and looked towards the
window as the mirrors were raised, spreading the dim
glow around the cavern.

'You know,' whispered Latisha, 'this reminds me of a
film I once saw about a fellow who gets trapped in a
horrible computer game. That's just how I feel. Is this
happening, Miriam, or are we all mad?' She got up and
went over to the window, the chains on her legs jangling as
she walked. Standing on her toes she peered out. 'Oh
cripes!' she exclaimed. 'The children.'

Miriam swept over to see. She pressed her hand to her
mouth to prevent herself from crying out as she saw Ed,
along with a line of other children, being ushered meekly
along the street. They disappeared into a building beyond
Elder Samuel's house. Miriam leaned against the wall. She
felt all her strength leave her body and, without any
warning, threw up.

'Oh, Miriam,' Latisha rushed to her sympathetically. But
Miriam waved her away. She retched again and again, but
there was nothing in her stomach. She wiped her mouth on
her sleeve and looked embarrassed.

'Sorry about that,' she muttered.

By now the boys were awake, looking at her with
concern.

'Miriam ...' began Lou.

'Please don't fuss,' she said. 'I'm all right. Leave me be.'

'Sit down,' said Latisha, guiding her back to the mattress
and putting one of the rugs around her.

Harry gritted his teeth. 'Sod this,' he said angrily. 'Let me open these chains now. Let's take our chances and rush those slimeballs. We can't take any more, Lou ...'

But Lou was shaking his head. 'Cool it, Harry,' he said. 'We've got to do this properly. Our only hope is that gas line that Ralph told us about. If one of us can follow that and get to civilisation and help, well, we're out of here. We mustn't rush bullheaded into a situation that'll make things worse.'

'Lou's right,' said Ralph. 'If we try something like that, there's no knowing what they might do ...'

'Shit!' swore Harry. 'It's my fault that we're here. If I hadn't gone back for that stupid silver thing ...'

'Oh give over, Harry,' put in Latisha. 'Ifs and buts don't make things any better. Anyway, it's hardly your fault that Ralph is here, or those kids who were taken down here. Let's keep sane, for goodness' sake.'

'Right,' agreed Lou. 'If we hadn't come here, those kids would never be found. We're going to get out, all of us. But we must do this properly.'

Ralph nodded his head. 'I think your best bet is to do as I do,' he said. 'Pretend to go along with these people. Make them think that you're impressed by whatever they're at. Lull them into thinking that you're no trouble. That's how I survived. They knew I'd never follow their cult, but I did whatever tasks they set me. That's how I got to get books and things ...'

'But you've been here for years for chrissake!' interrupted Harry. 'If you think I'd stay here for one week, skivvying meekly, then think again, sunshine.'

'Listen, Harry,' said Latisha. 'Nobody's going to stay here that long. We'll be out of here as soon as we can. But we must plan carefully. Go on, Ralph.'

'Like I said before,' continued Ralph, 'if we're back digging potatoes again today, we'll look for that entrance to the gas line. If one of us could somehow get near it, we could gauge its size. Later on, when we're back here, we can plan where we go from there.'

'Sounds pretty hairy,' grumbled Harry. 'Hopeless, in other words.'

'Have you something better in mind?' Lou asked scornfully.

Harry shook his head.

'Well then, let's do as Ralph says. If that passage is too small, we'll make other plans. Let's just take one thing at a time, however slim the chances.'

Miriam shivered and pulled the blanket about her.

'It does make sense,' said Latisha. 'It will be hard to act out. I mean it will take a lot of work to convince them that we're a harmless bunch of mousies.'

'Wee sleekit, cowerin' timorous beastie,' quoted Lou. 'What a panic ... dum di dum ...'

'Stop showing off, Lou,' Latisha smiled. 'We know you're a literary freak.'

'That's Burns,' Ralph looked up at Lou. 'Robbie Burns. So there is still poetry being taught in schools ...'

'Poetry!' scoffed Harry. 'We're trying to get out of this hell-hole and you talk about poetry!'

'We can't be talking misery all the time,' retorted Lou. 'A sense of balance is needed.'

'He's right,' agreed Ralph. 'A sense of balance is important. I know it's hard for you to realise that at this early stage - you've only been here a matter of hours. But keep a sense of balance in your minds. I should know - and I was here alone.'

'A sense of humour ...' began Latisha.

'Yes!' Ralph looked at her eagerly.

'Hell!' Harry threw up his hands. 'First poetry, now humour! What next? Bring on Rave music? I just want to get out of here.'

'Yes, Harry,' Latisha said patiently. 'And we will. But, as Ralph says, we must keep sane in the meantime and the only way we can do that is to be ... is to be as normal as possible.' She looked up slyly at Harry and grinned. 'I know "normal" is tough for you, Harry, but give it a try.'

'Stupid bunch of wrinklies,' he grunted. 'I hate to give them the satisfaction of thinking we're wimps.' He looked at Latisha and grinned. 'Okay. Let's do it that way - for a while.'The key scraped in the lock and two women brought

69

in food on trays.

Harry sniffed the concoction in the bowls and looked up at the men who stood by the door.

'I suppose bacon and egg is out of the question,' he said. They merely scowled before closing the door and locking it. 'Thought not,' Harry mumbled and then shouted after them, 'Vampires! Bet you all hang upside down at night.'

Latisha smiled, pleased at least that the old Harry was beginning to emerge. They ate in silence, each one wondering what today would bring.

They were barely given time to finish when their escorts were back to take them to work. Once again the boys were led towards the green area. Lou winked at Miriam and Latisha. At least that part of the plan was in order.

Latisha groaned as the wash house loomed again.

'Oh no. Not more stupid scrubbing,' she said. 'If I see another Victorian, heavy-duty knickers, I'll scream.'

Miriam nudged her. 'We've got to look like we don't mind,' she whispered. Latisha looked at her with a comical expression. 'I'd rather have my teeth pulled,' she hissed back.

The day wore on in a seemingly eternal round of steam and heat. The girls' hands were raw and blistered.

'If I do any more of this I'll have white hands,' said Latisha. 'That's all I need - honky hands.'

Miriam was rubbing the front of her sweater with a wet rag. 'I can't seem to get rid of the smell of vomit,' she said. 'I think I'll take a chance and dump my sweater in with the rest of the washing.' She whipped off the soiled, red sweater and threw it into the hot water. 'I can smuggle it back and dry it over the window.' She tucked her shirt into her jeans and immersed her hands in the water once more. She lifted up a shirt and looked at it with horror. Then she picked up another garment.

'Oh, no,' she moaned.

'What is it?' asked Latisha. 'Found a body?'

'It's run,' said Miriam. 'My sweater has run. The clothes are pink.'

'Oh, oh,' said Latisha, peering into Miriam's sink. 'You're

right. Everything's coming up roses.'

Miriam picked up more and more clothes. All of them were a bright shade of pink. The girls looked at one another with dismay. Then Miriam's mouth spread into a smile and both of them burst into uncontrollable laughter. Miriam leaned against the sink to balance herself. Latisha sank to the floor, holding her arm to her mouth to muffle her merriment. They both shook helplessly.

'Can you imagine?' Miriam spluttered when she'd got her breath back. 'Can you imagine all these zombies dressed in bright pink?'

Their laughter released all the recent pent up emotions. A glance or a gesture towards the offending pink washing sparked off more and more laughter.

'Oh Lord,' Latisha wiped her eyes eventually. 'They'll hang us.'

'Ssshhh,' said Miriam, nodding towards the door. It creaked open and the two women who were their guards entered. They stood for a moment, looking at the two girls. Miriam, still giddy from laughter, had a vision of the two grim women in pink undies. Once again she began to snigger.

'Sshh,' hissed Latisha, although she had put her sleeve to her mouth to hide a further attack of giggles. The older woman frowned disapprovingly, but said nothing. The other released the chain that was attached to Miriam's manacles.

'Come with us,' snapped the older one. Miriam looked anxiously at Latisha. Was it possible that these people had detected the runny wash already and that she was about to be punished? Was it more than their hearing that had become overdeveloped in all their years down here. As she was led through the door, she glanced back at Latisha standing forlornly at the sink, all laughter wiped away. Somehow she felt that things would never be the same again.

Thirteen

Knowing it would be futile to protest, Miriam accompanied the two women to a faded, run-down house beside the meeting hall. Inside, in a sparsely furnished room, Elder Samuel was sitting in a high-winged armchair. The room smelled of must and neglect, but it was clean. Faded curtains hung limply on the single window through which the cheerless light filtered, not quite reaching the dark corners. An old-fashioned clock, its face speckled with brown spots, ticked loudly across the silence.

The eyes in Elder Samuel's grey face lit up when Miriam was brought in. Beside him stood a middle-aged woman who put up her hand for Miriam to stop some distance away. The two other women took up position at the door. Fear gripped the back of Miriam's neck. She wished she hadn't been singled out, that the others were standing here with her. She'd never felt so isolated, so different in her life.

Samuel and the woman looked at her with cold interest, as if sizing up a side of beef, she thought, and spoke in low tones among themselves. Miriam felt her flesh creep as their eyes ate into her. She folded her arms and hunched her shoulders as if to hide herself from their gaze. She remembered the way that awful man had looked at her yesterday in the laundry and the fear sown in her mind then returned.

After a while Elder Samuel stood up. She watched in horror as he came towards her. To avoid his manic stare, she kept her eyes on the hoop of keys that dangled from his belt. He paused for a moment beside her and she braced herself, determined to scratch him if he so much as touched her. He bared his yellowed teeth in a grin and went out. Miriam sighed with relief as the tension left her. Now the woman was coming towards her. Reaching out a bony hand she pressed Miriam's hip.

'Don't you touch me,' hissed Miriam.

The woman shrugged. 'You are the lucky one,' she said.

Miriam recoiled. 'Lucky?'

The woman nodded. 'Elder Samuel is taking you as wife,' she said. 'You are of age. You will bear children ...'

Miriam put her hands over her ears. 'No!' she cried. 'Never. I'd kill myself before I'd let that creep come near me ...'

The woman shook her head. 'You will wed him,' she said more firmly. 'Either willingly or otherwise, he will take you as his bride. We have no young women left. You will provide heirs to carry on our way of life ...'

'No!' Miriam was looking at the woman in desperation. 'I won't do it. I won't.'

'It will be easier if you accept the will of Elder Samuel,' the woman continued. Miriam backed away as the woman brought her face closer. Her skin gathered in drippy folds under her eyes. Her lower teeth projected beyond the upper ones, adding to her grim expression. 'It will be easier for your friends,' she added ominously.

'No!' Miriam spat the word. 'You people are mad.'

The woman lashed out with her hand and dealt Miriam a stinging slap on the face. Miriam gasped.

'You can hit and bully all you like,' she said, her voice shaking. 'But you will never make me marry that old ...' she ducked as the hand lashed out again.

'I believe we have your brother among our Novice Dwellers.' The woman smiled in triumph at the flash of concern on Miriam's face. 'Just remember your brother and your friends. Remember this, girl, we have no need of your friends. Take her back,' she said to the other two. 'Let her think things over until later. Let her think of the consequences of her decision.'

In the meantime, Lou, Ralph and Harry were engaged in the backbreaking job of harvesting potatoes. Careful watch was kept on the three boys by the other harvesters. However, by careful manoeuvering, Lou managed to get near Ralph's drill. They didn't dare even whisper, but odd glances were enough to communicate the need to get near one another. Lou looked up when a clod of earth landed at his feet. Ralph glanced across at him and, with his eyes, indicated towards his left side. Lou nodded imperceptibly and followed Ralph's eyes. In the rough, stone side of the cave, at the edge of the green area, there was a low, narrow opening. From it several pipes wound their way towards the houses. Lou smiled. So this was the entrance to the gas line. He raised his hand, the accepted signal for wanting to relieve himself.

'Be quick,' growled the guard in charge of the boys. Lou made his way across the drills of potatoes until he came to the wall. He slipped behind a rock that was jutting out and quickly noted the size of the opening. He daren't explore further or he would arouse suspicion. He made his way back, nodding to Harry and then to Ralph. The three of them continued their task with renewed vigour; however slim their chances, at least there was the optimism of forming a plan to escape.

Fourteen

'Miriam!' Latisha rushed over to where Miriam was sitting on her own on the mattress. She and the boys had just returned from their work. 'What is it? You're as white as a sheet. What have they done? Have they hurt you? Did they find out about that stupid pink dye running?'

Miriam shook her head and clenched her fists until the knuckles were white. 'They say I've to ... to marry that mad creep, that Samuel.'

Latisha gasped. 'Oh, God!'

'What?' Lou leaned closer. 'Are you sure that's what they said?'

Miriam nodded. She wrapped her arms around her legs and rested her forehead on her knees. 'Could things get any worse than this?' she muttered.

Latisha reached out and smoothed Miriam's hair. There was no answer to that.

'When?' asked Lou.

Miriam looked up. 'There's no when,' she said. 'I won't do it. They want to use me to ... to bear his heirs. Can you imagine anything more disgusting than ... than ... ugghhh?' She let her head sink again. 'I will not do it. You must promise to kill me first.'

The others looked at one another over her shoulder. Their faces tensed as they realised that Miriam would have no control in this situation.

'They took me to this dreary house,' continued Miriam. 'That creep was there. He looked at me. Just sat there and looked at me,' she twisted her mouth in disgust. 'Then his sidekick, an old ratbag, told me that ...' she looked up at the others. 'She told me that it would be better for my friends and my brother if I ... I agreed to go along with their wishes. Where does that leave me? How can I make choices like that?'

'There is no choice, Miriam,' said Lou. 'We'll stick together for as long as we're here. Don't agree to anything. Stick to your guns. They can't make you marry. They can't.'

'That's right,' agreed Latisha.

'But what about you people and Ed?' asked Miriam, miserably. 'Won't they do something awful to you if I don't agree?'

'Idle threat,' said Harry. 'Don't mind that.'

Miriam wasn't at all convinced, but it was good to know that the others were on her side. Lou put his hand on her shoulder.

'Don't worry, Miriam,' he said. 'It's time for action. We'll get out of here. We've seen the entrance where the gas pipes go, so now we can plan.'

'Keep your voices right down,' warned Ralph. 'Don't forget these people have amazing hearing.'

The five of them huddled closer together.

'Harry, are you sure you can open these chains?' asked Lou.

'Child's play,' Harry grinned.

'What about the lock on the door?' asked Ralph. Harry got up and went over to the door. Pressing himself against the keyhole, he peered through it.

'I could do it with a bit of wire,' he said. 'It's an old-fashioned ward lock.'

'A what?' Latisha asked.

'A ward lock. It probably has only one tumbler ...'

'Harry will you stop talking like a con and tell us whether you can open it or not,' hissed Lou.

Harry grinned. 'Can do,' he said. 'But I'll need a bit of wire.'

Ralph was rummaging under his mattress. He drew out a spring.

'How about this?' he said.

Harry took it from him and tried to smooth out the coils.

'Give me a hand,' he said. The others took turns in trying to straighten out the piece of wire.

'Hide it,' Latisha whispered, pointing towards the door.

They watched as the door opened and food was brought in.

'McDonald's burgers and fries,' Harry said in an effort to keep up a normal front. It was difficult to suppress the excitement they all were feeling right now.

When the two women had left, they returned to their huddle.

'Okay,' said Harry. 'It's straight enough now. What's next?'

They looked at Ralph for guidance.

'Who's going? You people are probably fitter than me. I'm afraid I've picked up the dreaded lung condition,' he admitted. 'I haven't run for so many years ... If it came to a chase ...'

'Me,' said Harry. 'I'll go.'

'No. I'm going,' put in Lou.

'Why should it be you?' Harry looked offended. 'Don't you trust me?'

'Oh, cool it, Harry. It's not that,' explained Lou. 'I've seen the opening. I know where to go. Besides if, as Ralph says, the place where the pipes join up with the town pipes is very narrow, I'd have a better chance of squeezing through than you. You're skinny, but there's too much of you to fit through narrow openings. You're all arms and legs.'

'Then I'll come with you,' said Harry.

'Lou's right,' said Ralph. 'We don't know what's down that tunnel. A smaller person has a better chance.'

Harry grunted and hit the air with his fists.

They ate their warm porridge before the women returned.

'Now,' said Ralph when they'd collected the bowls. 'There will be no more interruptions for the night. After their own meal, they'll go as usual to the meeting hall for Elder Samuel's nightly sermon. That's the time to act. Everyone goes to that. Especially now that they think we're a docile lot.'

'How will we know when they've all gone in?' asked Lou.

'About ten minutes after the mirrors are drawn in,' said Ralph. 'That should be safe enough.'

'Go straight to the police, once you get out,' said Latisha. 'Don't stop to tell parents or anyone. Just get help straight away.'

77

'You don't have to tell me that, Latisha,' Lou snapped. 'I'm not a fool.'

'Sorry,' Latisha said. 'I didn't mean it like that.'

'Cool it, folks,' said Miriam. 'We're all up in a heap. Keep calm. If this doesn't work I become the bride of Dracula.' She tried to be humorous, but the shake in her voice betrayed her anxiety.

They all froze as, with the clanking and squeaking of pulleys, the mirrors were drawn in. It was time. Lou paled and turned to Harry who knelt down to unlock his chains. Miriam handed Lou his torch from under the mattress.

'Good job we managed to hold on to this,' she said. She looked at his tense face and wished she could say something reassuring, something encouraging, but words would sound false at this time. Instead she shyly gave him a hug.

They waited in strained silence until they heard the first chanting coming from the meeting hall. Lou took a deep breath as he and Harry went to the door. Ralph and Latisha kept watch at the window. After what seemed like eternity, the lock clicked gently and Harry eased open the door. With one last look, Lou slipped out into the quiet street. Harry re-locked the door and turned to the others. 'Now the long wait,' he said.

Fifteen

Lou paused before slipping into the shadows. He moved easily behind the derelict houses, keeping out of sight of the meeting hall. Now and then he looked back to see if he was being pursued, but the sounds of singing from the meeting house reassured him that there was nobody following. Even with their super hearing, they couldn't possible hear his stealthy movements over that din.

'Keep in the shadows,' Ralph had warned. 'Stay well behind the old houses.'

The street was still empty. Lou took a deep breath and continued on. The light got weaker as he went beyond the street area, and soon it was almost dark. Still it was too risky to switch on the torch. He came to the green area and felt his way along the wall. He knew the entrance was about half way along the length of the potato patch.

At last his hand felt the jutting rock where he'd hidden earlier today. Another few yards and he was in the tunnel. He went in as far as he could without light. He felt the pipes which ran along one side. Lou smiled. All he had to do was to follow the pipes.

'Just lead me to the real world,' he breathed.

There was a chill dampness which he felt through his sweatshirt; he'd given his t-shirt to Harry. It had been very tempting to bring Harry along, but it made better sense to come alone. If it was at all possible to find a way through this gas line, then one had a better chance.

The cave narrowed into a crude tunnel which was supported by timber buttresses along the way. It seemed to stretch into an eternity of yawning nothingness. Lou turned on his torch and was relieved that it was still working. He would have to leave it on. Anyway, all being well, he wouldn't be coming back this way so he wouldn't need it.

Now the tunnel was little more than shoulder high and Lou had to walk with a stoop. It was eerie and claustrophobic down there.

If I stop to think about being trapped in this tiny, black space, thought Lou, I'll get the screaming jitters. It was like those stories he used to read about little boys who were forced by chimney sweeps to climb up narrow flues to clear away the soot. Some of them died of suffocation. Sometimes, after reading such stories, Lou would turn off his light and crawl under the bedclothes, pretending to be one of those boys. He always came up gasping and quickly turned on the comforting bedside light. Only this time there were no bedclothes and no bedside light. This was real and it was awful. Something scurried across the top of the tunnel and Lou's heart leapt.

'Bloody hell!' he swore softly when the torchlight picked out a huge spider. 'That's all I need.' Instinctively he brushed himself down in case any more of those things might have landed on him.

By now he was wishing that the others were with him. 'Get real, Lou,' he told himself. 'Don't let this place get to you.' In the first place they would probably all be missed immediately and hotly pursued. It was better that they were behind, making sounds, making their presence felt so that there would be no suspicion.

He tried to think of optimistic things. What would he do when he got out? He would quickly go to the police. No doubt everyone's parents were sick with worry at this stage.

He imagined his Mum and Dad organising search parties and staying by the phone all night in case any news came in. How many times had Mum talked sympathetically about those missing children, little realising that her own son would be one of them. Funny, it was always Lou's younger brother and sister who were given dire warnings about strangers and told to go about in groups. Probably felt I was old enough to look after myself, he thought wryly. He tried to visualise his Dad's face, but, no matter how much he concentrated, the image would not come right.

He wondered what day it was. Was it Sunday? Were they only down here two days? It felt like forever. On

Sunday nights he and Dad went bowling. It was their special time together. Part of that weekly ritual was to stop off at McDonalds for burgers and milkshakes; always chocolate for Dad. Funny how all the things that you took for granted seemed so precious when whipped away from you. Lou swallowed hard. If he ever got out of this ... dammit he had to get out of this. All those kids back there were depending on him.

The tunnel was now so low that Lou had to crawl. He had to fight back the panic that crept up the back of his neck. Now he wished more than anything that Harry was here. Perhaps he should go back. If he returned now the Dwellers would be in bed and would not have missed him. Pull yourself together, he told himself, gritting his teeth and wiping sweat off his glasses.

When he thought that it could get no narrower, his torch picked out something metallic embedded in the side wall. A different sort of gaspipe! A single large one. Lou banged his head against the top of the tunnel with the excitement. It had to lead to a major pipeline soon. At least he was on the right track. Thank goodness he hadn't given up. He sighed and soldiered on.

The tunnel twisted sharply now and there was a junction joint on the pipe. A bit farther on there was another one. The junction was shiny and had tool marks on it. Obviously repairs had been done there recently. 'Please let it lead to the source,' he prayed. He tried to keep his optimism at bay as he neared the bend. Round he crawled and shone the torch ahead.

His heart fell as he was confronted by a solid grey door embedded into the wall. The pipe disappeared through a hole in the door. Tears of disappointment welled up in Lou's eyes. He hammered the wall of the tunnel in frustration. Had he now to crawl all the way back along this suffocating tunnel and confront the others with the heartbreaking news that there was no way out? He crawled closer to the door. It was heavy wood.He pounded on it, but the sound was just a muffled thump. He shone the torch along the bottom. Hang on, he thought, the wood at the end of the door seemed quite splintered. He felt it and some splinters came away in his hand. He took a breath. There might be a way out after all. He picked at the wood and more of it came off. If he could just make an opening large enough to crawl through, he'd be into the next tunnel. That had to be where the main gas line ran. The wood was indeed quite rotten and had a sort of mushroom smell.

After an eternity of scrabbling and pulling the wood, Lou felt a draught of air. He was through! He put his eye to the hole and shone the torch through. All he could see was more blackness. Well, at least it appeared to be a bigger tunnel than this one. He might even be able to walk erect. By now his fingernails were broken and bloody, but Lou didn't seem to notice.

Gradually the hole got bigger. Lou paused for breath. He was exhausted and the air was very bad. He wondered if there was any oxygen at all, or had he been breathing the same breath in and out for the past few hours! Not much more to go. He grunted as the sweat dripped into his eyes and his glasses fogged up.

There! Quite a sizeable hole now appeared at the bottom of the door. He bent as low as he could and peered through. There was a distant hum. Could that be some sort of generator? Would they have a generator in a place like this? Of course they would. They would have to have electric light for maintenance purposes. That meant that somewhere close by there was civilisation. Lou was so excited he wanted to go through immediately. He removed a few more slivers of the rotten wood and deemed the hole large enough to take him.

He took off his sweater and pushed it through. Then he took the torch and wormed his way into the hole. Wow! he was indeed in a much larger tunnel. There were pipelines going everywhere. Modern, plastic looking pipes. Pipes put there by people from Above - there he was using that silly word. He smiled and eased himself in a bit further. He shone the light upwards and gasped in awe at the cleverness of the Dwellers. Their pipe was concealed at the back of the much larger supply pipe. One would never know it was there because the wooden door had been painted to look like rock. In fact, on this side, the rock almost covered the doorway.

Lou dug his elbows into the earth and heaved himself another few inches. His chest was clear. God, it was a tight squeeze. Another bit. He expelled all the air from his lungs and gripped the earth on the tunnel floor. Nothing happened. He let his head fall on to the floor as he gathered some more strength. He gritted his teeth and heaved once more. There was a very slight give and then nothing. He could feel the waves of panic begin to envelop him again. 'I must get through,' he whispered. He wriggled and squirmed, but not another inch did he move. The logical thing, he told himself as he fought down the panic, was to ease back out and enlarge the hole.

'Easy does it,' he gasped. But he could not lever himself back. Fear finally overcame him and he struck about frantically with legs and fists. With a black, mortal dread, he realised he was well and truly stuck under a heavy door in a tunnel miles beneath the earth with not a soul about to help him. It was at that moment that the torch batteries finally gave up.

Sixteen

'I should have gone with him,' Harry said. Several hours had elapsed since Lou slipped away. The four who were left behind huddled together in the shadows of the detention house. Miriam shivered; she missed her sweater which was still in the wash place, and pulled the thin blanket tighter around her.

'No Harry,' Latisha was saying. 'We've been through that. If it can be managed at all, Lou will get through. There's got to be a place where those gas pipes meet up with the town supply. There's got to be.'

Sleep was out of the question in the tense atmosphere of anxiety and helplessness. Every so often Harry got up and paced about, his chains rattling off the hard floor. He had wanted to take them off, to take off all their chains, but Ralph insisted that they should stay on.

'If they come in for any reason,' he said, 'they'll suspect nothing when they see our legs still chained. That,' he nodded to where they had rolled up a bundle of rags and put them on a mattress deep in the shadows, 'that will fool them into thinking it's Lou - at least for the time being. But we must be very careful to behave completely as normal to give Lou plenty of time.'

Miriam sighed. 'Do you think Lou will get back with help before I get to be dragged ...?'

'Ssshhh, Miriam. Don't talk like that,' said Latisha. 'There's no way you'll be the Bride of Dracula. We won't let them take you.' But her words convinced no one.

'I wish they'd let me see my brother,' went on Miriam. 'Those kids - they're all so quiet. You'd imagine that they'd be shouting and bawling, yet all they do is go meekly into that schoolroom or whatever it is. I keep expecting to hear Ed shouting and causing a fuss. What do they say to them to keep them so quiet?'

'Laudanum,' said Ralph.

'What?'

'Laudanum. It's a potion based on opium. They use it to

calm people - I've seen people almost go mad when they become ill. They know there's no cure and that they'll die. I've also seen women who've had dead babies. They go crazy with grief. Times like that the laudanum is administered. It's precious stuff and Elder Samuel is the only one with the key to the cupboard where it's kept. He has the keys of everywhere.'

'What's all this got to do with the children?' asked Miriam.

'Well,' said Ralph. 'I'd say they're administering some to them to keep them calm until they settle.'

'Oh God!' exclaimed Latisha. 'You mean they're drugging them?'

Ralph shrugged. 'In a way, yes.'

'Pervert bloody pushers,' growled Harry.

Miriam was thoughtful for a few moments. 'Do you mean that, if someone were to start throwing tantrums and stuff, they'd give them that stuff to calm them down?'

Ralph nodded. Latisha looked anxiously at Miriam; she knew what was running through her mind. No matter what kind of fuss Miriam might make, when the time came for her to be brought before Elder Samuel, they would force that stuff down her throat.

'There's somebody coming!' exclaimed Harry, rushing back from the window. There were voices and scuffles outside. The four youngsters tensed as the door was flung open. They recoiled with horror as Lou was pushed in roughly and fell to the floor. He looked so pathetic as he crouched there; he was naked from the waist up and his face and upper body were covered in grime and scratches. His glasses were cracked and dirty. Around his neck he still had that ridiculous dog whistle. Miriam grabbed a blanket and ran over to him, trying not to trip over her chains.

Lou raised himself on his arms. 'I'm sorry,' he almost sobbed. 'I'm so sorry.'

'It's all right,' soothed Miriam as she wrapped the blanket around him. She fought back the hopeless panic that this moment had brought. 'You were very brave to try it ...'

'No,' Lou wiped his face on a corner of the blanket. 'I'm
so furious. I was within that,' he snapped his fingers, 'of
civilisation. I'd got as far as the tunnel which leads to the
outer network of gaspipes. I could hear the generator ... I
was that close.'

'What happened?' asked Harry.

'I got stuck, didn't I!' said Lou angrily. 'I got bloody
stuck. I've let you all down ... I shouted and shouted in the
hopes that someone up there would hear me. But no,' he
spat bitterly. 'The only ones who heard were these ... these
weirdoes with their weird hearing. They heard me all
right. Scumbags!'

'Shush,' said Latisha. 'You tried. We'll think of
something else.'

'No,' Lou was shaking his head with a defeated air. 'No.
They're in a dangerous mood. They won't allow this to
happen again. I've been listening to them.'

'What do you mean?' asked Latisha.

Miriam realised now what the woman in Elder Samuel's
house had meant. She'd said 'we have no need of your
friends'. She anticipated Lou's next words with dread.

Lou hesitated.

'For chrissake spit it out, Lou,' snapped Harry.

Lou looked up at the white faces. 'They want rid of us,'
he said.

Latisha slapped her hand to her mouth and closed her
eyes. Harry looked incredulous. Ralph was nodding
slowly, as if he'd expected Lou's words. Miriam watched
Lou sink back on his heels, his bony body half out of the
blanket she'd put around him. In spite of the terrifying
situation, she wanted to put her arms around him and
comfort him; chatty, brainy Lou who'd risked so much for
all of them.

None of them slept during what remained of the night.
Now and then someone would make an attempt at
discussing the awful predicament, but matters had gone
beyond words. Miriam lay staring at the wooden planks on
the ceiling, each one running in a straight line to the other

side of the room. If only life could run in a straight line, she thought. Start at birth and run smoothly to the end. The mellow wood had an oddly calming effect on her, helping to steer her thoughts beyond panic to careful reasoning. By the time the key turned in the lock the next morning, she knew what she must do.

Seventeen

When the door opened again in the morning, it was not to bring food. Five men stood menacingly, sticks poised in their hands. The youngsters shrank back on the mattress. Except for Miriam. She stood up and faced the men.

'Tell Elder Samuel that I'll ... that I'll agree to go to him willingly.' She wished her voice wouldn't shake so much. The men looked taken aback for an instant, but then they advanced into the room, ignoring her statement. One of them prodded Lou with his stick.

'Move,' he said. 'All of you move. Follow.'

Miriam caught his arm and he tried to shrug her off.

'Elder Samuel wants me to be his bride,' she persisted her voice rising. 'You must go and tell him that I'll come willingly if he leaves these people alone. Tell him. If you don't ... if he finds out that I'd have come willingly before you ... before you do whatever you intend to do, then he'll be extremely angry.'

She heard Latisha's voice saying 'No, Miriam. Don't do it. Don't give in!' But Miriam kept her eyes focused on the man who appeared to be the leader of this bunch.

'Go and tell him,' Miriam said, her voice now more even. The man looked dubious for a moment. Then he turned to one of the others.

'Fetch Elder Samuel,' he said.

'Don't do this, Miriam,' Lou caught her by the arm. 'Whatever happens, we're sticking together.'

'Quiet, boy!' One of the men pushed Lou away.

'Back off, prat,' Harry sized up to the man, his long, skinny arms in an aggressive position. Miriam didn't look at her companions. She knew if she did that the plans she'd made during the night might be jeopardised by emotion. She stared coldly ahead. She felt her reserve almost give way when the messenger returned with Elder Samuel. He seemed to have decayed even more than when she saw him last. He cast his steely glance around the tense group and then looked questioningly at the leader of the men.

'You want me as your bride,' said Miriam. The words seemed to be coming from someone else, she thought. Could she really be saying this?

'I'll agree to that. I'll willingly go along with that if you will leave these friends of mine alone.'

Elder Samuel's face broke into a sickening, yellow-toothed grin. He leaned forward and touched Miriam's face. She flinched and Harry made a move towards Elder Samuel. Latisha caught his arm and pulled him back.

'So, you will be my bride after all,' the grey-faced Elder was saying. 'Very well.' He nodded to the men. 'Let these prisoners stay. You come along with me, my dear,' he pointed a bony finger at Miriam.

Miriam cast a brief, backward glance at her friends before being led out. She was once again overcome by a terrible isolation, but there was some comfort in knowing that her bid for time had worked.

The others looked at one another after the door was locked.

'She's cool,' said Harry. 'She did that to save us.'

But nobody was fooled for a moment by Elder Samuel's ready capitulation to Miriam's terms.

'Once he has Miriam in his greasy grasp, it'll be curtains for us,' said Lou.

'I know, but it gives us a little more time.'

'Time for what?' asked Lou, bitterly. 'I've fouled up our only hope. There's nothing else.'

Harry thumped the mattress in frustration. 'Let's just rush them,' he said. 'Let's go out there and fight them with everything we've got ...'

'What have we got, Harry?' said Ralph, with calm reasoning. 'We have yourself and Lou - two mere boys, Latisha - feisty but no match for these brutes. And me - unfit, undernourished, wheezy and about as useful as a straw in the wind.'

'We've got to do something,' said Harry.

'Ralph's right,' sighed Lou. 'Let's wait ...'

'Ah, wait my foot!' scoffed Harry. 'Take them on, I say.'

'We will wait, Harry,' said Latisha. 'If it comes to ... to

them trying to waste us, then we'll go down fighting. But, until then, we must be patient. Remember there's Miriam and that bunch of kids in this as well. We have to consider them too.'

Harry's face crumpled in frustration and he sat down heavily.

'If only they hadn't blown up that tunnel,' said Lou. 'If only we still had that way out.'

Miriam was handed over to the two women who had supervised herself and Latisha in the wash-house. She wondered, briefly, if they'd found the pink washing yet. She resolved to be docile, to go along with whatever they wanted her to do. This would give her every opportunity to observe anything that might help escape. It was all up to her now. She sighed and let herself be led into one of the houses. Like Elder Samuel's, it was clean and sparsely furnished.

A stuffed pheasant looked at her, glassy-eyed, from a dusty dome. It occurred to her that these people would never have seen a live bird nor heard birdsong - their only concept of something beautiful was this moth-eaten dead thing in a glass dome that had been brought down with the first settlers. A single faded picture on the wall depicted a rural landscape, another tragic reminder of life before this cult was conceived and a sad reminder to Miriam of a world beyond this madness.

The knots on the wooden floor were shiny from years of footsteps. The light from a smelly oil lamp threw a soft glow around the dreary room.

'I will be downstairs,' the older woman said, casting a suspicious glance at Miriam.

Miriam grimaced. 'I'm not about to attack anyone,' she muttered.

'I'll be all right, Sarah,' said the second woman. 'You get on with your arrangements.'

Miriam turned her back on the two women and concentrated on keeping calm.

'Take off your clothes,' the remaining woman said as the door closed after her departing sidekick. In spite of her earlier decision to be docile, Miriam was defensive.

'I will not,' she retorted, clutching her shirt. It was bad enough being isolated from the company of her friends, but she was damned if she was going to be robbed of her identity completely.

'You cannot be part of our people dressed like that,' the woman pointed to Miriam's shirt and jeans. 'Please put on this dress.'

It was the word *please* that made Miriam look at the woman's face. She was surprised to see an expression of fear rather than hostility on the woman's face. Although she was thin and haggard, with a complexion like raw dough, she was really quite young. She looked anxiously towards the door as she shook out a brown dress. Miriam sensed that the young woman wanted to speak, but was unsure of how to begin. Miriam decided to test the ground herself - an ally, however weak, would be a bonus in this hostile place.

'What's your name?' she asked.

The young woman looked startled at being asked a direct question. She flustered about, spreading the dress on the bed and fluffing out the skirt.

So much for friendly vibes, thought Miriam bitterly. You're on your own, old girl.

'Lucy.' It was almost a whisper. Miriam wondered if she'd heard properly.

'What?' she said.

'Lucy,' the girl said again. 'Lucy Ambrose is my name.'

Miriam sighed. It was a very small victory but very significant. There was so much she wanted to say to this girl, to reach out for any shred of consolation she might offer.

'What is it like?' Lucy asked, before Miriam could speak. 'Up there, what is it like?'

'It's ... it's okay,' replied Miriam. Stupid response, she realised, but how do you describe your world to someone who hasn't seen it? Where do you begin? 'We have cars and televisions and we've had men landing on the moon,' she said. She began to explain about the huge leaps in technology, but Lucy interrupted her.

'The people,' she said. 'tell me about the people. What are they like?'

Miriam stopped and stared at the girl. All this incredible technology and Lucy simply wanted to know about the people.

'What about them?' Miriam asked. 'People are people.'

Lucy was shaking her head. 'Are there wars? Are people good to one another? Have machines destroyed humanity like Elder Samuel says?'

Miriam drew back at the rush of questions. 'I ... yes, there are wars,' she began. 'Wars all over the place, in fact.' Funny, she'd never really thought about the conflicts in the world before and now it seemed, in telling this girl, that the world was pretty singed from warfare. 'Mostly in countries far away,' she added lamely.

'But people are being killed,' went on Lucy. She sat on the bed beside the brown dress and looked up at Miriam. 'Soldiers?'

Miriam felt uneasy at the questions. She had wanted to tell this girl about the wonders of science, to see her eyes widen in wonder at the discoveries and inventions of mankind since her lot sought refuge down here.

'Soldiers, yes,' she replied. And people on streets, she thought. Babies in creches, children in schools, patients in hospitals, ordinary people who had no wish for war, but she couldn't bring herself to say so. It would be letting the world down. Better to gloss over those things.

'And the towns,' went on Lucy. 'Tell me about the towns. I often wish,' she paused and looked guilty at confessing to a stranger her secret thoughts, 'I often think it must be nice up there, living in houses with lots of neighbours all around. It must be so ... so safe and so much fun.'

Miriam began to take off her shirt and jeans. Lucy handed her the dress. It had been made for someone with a tinier wasit and Miriam had to breathe deeply to fasten the side buttons. it smelled of must and was probably damp. I'll probably catch cold from this, she thought. Her mother was always warning her about the consequences of wearing damp clothes. Then she smiled grimly at the irony of being worried about a head cold when her whole life, and the lives of others were at stake.

'Are they beautiful?' asked Lucy.

'What?'

'The towns, are they beautiful?'

'They're okay,' replied Miriam. 'And we don't actually know our neighbours. Not yet. We're not long in the place I live in now.' But then she hadn't really known her neighbours in her last area either. Mum and Dad's friends were from other parts of town and her own pals had been from school or ballet class or the tennis club. Before meeting Latisha and the others, that is. 'Some parts of town are nice,' she went on. 'The shopping mall, that's an area where shops are grouped together ...'

'A street?' said Lucy. 'I understand streets.'

'Well, sort of,' agreed Miriam. 'Anyway, that's mostly where friends meet. But you couldn't be in town late at night. It's a bit dangerous. People get stabbed and robbed. Fights break out ...'

'It's not safe?' Lucy put her hands to her mouth. 'People fight?'

Miriam shrugged. This was not the picture she wanted to paint of the world she knew. 'It's pretty cool - I mean all right - as long as you stick to the places you know,' she said. 'Look,' she added almost crossly, 'why are you asking all these questions? Your people decided to come down here all those years ago. Maybe they were right.' She felt confused and annoyed at the direction the conversation had taken. She wanted to be angry with Lucy, to accuse her and her people of the most awful kidnapping crimes, but all she was doing was getting her own lines crossed about life Above.

'We're safe,' said Lucy. 'There's no war down here. We live in peace.'

'And you're dying in peace,' said Miriam. 'All of you.'

'Which is better?' asked Lucy.

Miriam looked at the girl sharply and realised that this was a genuine question. Its simplicity threw her. She tried to imagine Lucy and all the other inhabitants of this bizarre place trying to adapt to a world where street-cred was the basis of survival and where rural fortification had taken the place of open-door hospitality, where the way you worshipped could be a one-way ticket to violent death. 'I don't know,' she said honestly. 'But I'd sooner take my chances in the fresh air.'

Lucy was about to say something but a look of alarm crossed her face as footsteps announced someone coming up the bare, wooden stairs. She busied herself, helping Miriam to do up her buttons.

'Is she ready?' asked the older woman, her skirts rustling as she crossed the floor.

'What's with the *she*,' hissed Miriam. 'I can answer for myself.'

The woman ignored her and took her arm. Miriam wrenched herself away, glad to be able to vent her frustration.

'Don't touch me,' she said. 'I'm not going anywhere.'

Lucy looked anxiously at her and Miriam winked. Lucy didn't respond. The friendly moment had passed.

Miriam was led to the house which she now knew to be Elder Samuel's. As before, he was sitting in state in his winged armchair. The same woman stood by his side. Didn't she ever sit?

'Ah,' he bared those teeth again. 'How nice you look, my dear,' he said. The woman nodded approvingly. Miriam concentrated on trying very hard not to throw up again.

'We shall have our union blessing this evening after worship,' Elder Samuel was saying. 'Sarah and Lucy will prepare you for the ceremony. I am pleased that you have seen the path of righteousness and that you are willing to serve our beliefs. You have made a wise decision.'

Miriam bit her lip and nodded. Tonight! A few short hours away. Only a miracle could save her from ... she looked at the deathly face that confronted her and tried to keep nightmare images from her mind.

The only small consolation that presented itself was the thought that, if there was to be a wedding ceremony, then

94

it surely meant that this creep would not put his greasy hands on her until after the ritual. Victorian religious freaks were probably fussy about all that stuff, she told herself. Time. A little more time.

Eighteen

'I would like to see my brother,' Miriam said, with as much confidence as she could muster.

The woman at Elder Samuel's side frowned and indicated to the others to remove Miriam. But Miriam stood firm. 'There is no harm in my intentions,' she said carefully. 'I merely want to see my brother, to tell him that I am to be the bride of Elder Samuel and that I will look after his needs.'

Elder Samuel held up his hand to silence the woman who had begun to protest.

'Of course, my dear,' he said, baring his teeth again. 'You tell him that if he co-operates, like his sister, there will be many rewards. Tell him that you will be in a position to see to his needs and the needs of those other Novice Dwellers. Tell him that, all together, we will resurrect the beliefs of our noble ancestors.' He nodded to the two women. 'See that the girl has everything she wants,' he added. 'See that she rests before our evening ceremony. Now, leave.'

Miriam clenched her fists as she left. So far so good. But so far yet to go. She took deep breaths like her mother had taught her when she was going through her yoga period. Mum was always involved in some mind-bending exercise like yoga or reflexology or t'ai chi. Mum. She dismissed the vision of her mother's face from her mind. That would lead to tears and there was no time for that. She looked up desperately at the high roof of the cave. If only she could see the sky, know that the real world existed out there. Just a glimpse of sky, a breath of air, a feeling of hope. Something stirred in her memory and she frowned as she tried to recall it. Sky. A patch of sky. Then it dawned on her. That time, after the explosion when they'd tried to run away, as hands pulled her back she had looked up and seen a small patch of sky above the rubble. The memory jolted her so much that she almost stumbled.

Out there in that tunnel there was a tiny opening!

Rough hands pushed her and she regained her

composure. The image of that tiny patch of sky stayed with her as she was led to the schoolhouse. The man at the head of the classroom looked up with surprise when the trio entered. The frightened children hardly lifted their eyes from their books at the interruption. Miriam understood why when she saw the bamboo cane wielded by the man. The women called Sarah spoke to him. Then Miriam's heart leapt when Ed was removed from his seat and led towards her. He too was dressed in old-fashioned clothing. He looked sleepy and disinterested. Miriam realised that he was tranquilised by ... what was that stuff that Ralph had spoken of? Loud ... loud ... laudanum. That was it.

She bent down and hugged her brother. Recognition dawned on his face.

'Miriam,' he whispered. 'Is it really you, Miriam?'

Miriam nodded, keeping a tight grip on him.

'We've got to get out of here, Ed,' she whispered closely in his ear. He backed away and looked at her.

'What?' he said loudly.

Miriam frowned at him and hugged him close again. She looked pleadingly at Lucy. Lucy gave a slight nod and turned to where Sarah and the teacher were talking. She joined in their conversation. Thank God, thought Miriam. However thin it was, a bond had been made between herself and this girl from another age. Please let her talk loudly enough to drown my whispers, she prayed. 'Don't drink,' she pressed her lips to Ed's ear. 'Whatever you do, don't drink anything they give you. Are you listening to me? Tell the other children. They mustn't drink anything, you understand? Look at me and nod that you understand. You drink nothing and you tell the others to drink nothing. But don't let any of these people hear you. Got that?'

Ed looked at her and nodded. God, thought Miriam, he looks like a robot. Has he understood anything? But the visit was over. Ed was led back to his desk and the two women took Miriam's arm. She was taken back to the house and was locked in. Through the window she could see the preparations for the wedding ritual. Women's lib hasn't reached this place, she thought as she watched the womenfolk bring out tables into the street. Obviously the ceremony would be open-air - if you could call it that down in this hell-hole. One particular table was set apart from the others. Candles were laid on it in elaborate holders. 'The high altar,' she said aloud. 'The sacrificial altar. Oh, God. Don't let me think of that bizarre ceremony.' It was like a setting for some satanic cult.

All day people went back and forth, carrying dishes and more candles, a heavy book was placed on a lectern in the middle of the street. Pitchers of wine were laid out in abundance; they must make their own, she thought. Probably potato wine. An Addams Family street party - she tried to hold on to her sanity with humour - only it wasn't a party, it was a sacrifice and she was it.

In the evening Miriam was brought some food - bread, and a glass of goat's milk. When she was alone, she ate the bread, but poured the milk through a hole in the floorboards. It was probably spiked with laudanum, she thought, to ensure she was a passive and willing bride. 'Yecchh,' she said aloud.

She stood at the window, watching the action below. She imagined that this was how prisoners must have felt long ago, sitting in their cells listening to the gallows being erected for their execution.

The room she was in gave her a good view of the street. On the right was the detention house. She thought longingly of her friends. Like them, she knew that their stay of execution was very temporary. She shuddered and tried not to think of their deaths, nor of her living death afterwards. Think of that patch of sky, she told herself. If only they could get to that patch of sky. But how? She peered up at the fading light from the mirrors. Very little time left now. Her hands were damp with sweat.

The schoolhouse door opened and the children trooped out, silent and submissive. She strained against the glass to see where they were led. They were ushered around the side of a house further up the street. Within a few moments, the man with the bamboo cane returned. He must have locked them in for the night, she thought.

Miriam backed away from the window. 'The poor little sods,' she whispered. When she heard footsteps outside, she quickly slipped over to the bed and lay down. She must pretend to be sleepy in case that milk had been spiked. She closed her eyes. Lucy and Sarah entered quietly, carrying an oil lamp. One of them raised it over Miriam's head. Something prompted her not to overact. She opened her eyes slowly.

'You must rest before the ceremony,' Sarah said.

Miriam nodded. 'Please leave me the lamp,' she said. 'I want to brush my hair.' She held her breath as the woman hesitated, and looked at Lucy. Lucy nodded and the older woman set the lamp beside the bed. Then they both set about laying out underclothes, shoes and a faded lace gown. Sacrificial robes, thought Miriam. She reached out and turned up the wick to get a stronger light. The reaction of the two women was astounding. With a shriek they shielded their eyes from the sudden increased light. Sarah blindly waved her hand and shouted to Miriam to turn it down. Shocked by their behaviour, Miriam turned the wick right down.

'Sorry,' she said. This was a revelation. The logic of it hit her like a slap - these people were so used to living in the half light of their underground existence that their eyes could not cope with bright light.

The clanking outside announced the withdrawal of the mirrors. It was time for evening worship. And then ... Miriam swallowed and watched the two women prepare to leave. Her stomach sank with a sickening, hopeless jolt.

'You will dress,' Sarah indicated the clothes. 'We shall come to fetch you after evening worship.'

Miriam remembered to appear drugged; she nodded sleepily. Lucy turned at the door. Her look was one of sympathy and helplessness. Miriam wanted to shout out to her, to ask her to stay here with her and help her through all this. She felt panic as the door closed. She sat on the bed for a moment. 'Move Miriam,' she said out loud. 'You've got to move your butt.' She slipped over to the window. All of the Dwellers were walking in slow procession to the meeting hall. She saw Elder Samuel come towards the hall. He was wearing a black suit. The trousers were knee breeches that showed off his wasted calf muscles. Miriam gritted her teeth; was there no end to this man's ugliness? Then she noticed that there was something else different. What was it? His face was the same, his hat was the same. Same waistcoat. Then she realised what it was. No keys! The hoop of keys that he always had around his waist was missing. He must have left them off in honour of the ceremony! She leaned back against the wall. If only she could lay her hands on those keys. She sank onto the bed. The keys and the patch of sky, those two images turned around and around in her mind. Keys and sky. The chanting had now begun. The evening worship was under way.

Nineteen

Over in the detention house, Latisha was standing on her toes, looking out at the activity.

'Poor Miriam,' she muttered. 'They're getting ready for the wedding. Oh, God. This is too awful!'

Ralph nodded. 'Once they have her under their control ...'

'Stop!' Latisha tried to keep her panic at bay. 'How do you think they'll ... they'll ...?' She turned her big eyes on Ralph.

'Probably poison,' he said.

'Listen to you two!' cried Harry. He was pressed against the door trying to peer through the grille at the outside padlock that had been put on since Lou's escape. How many times had he tried to reach it before giving up the exercise as totally useless? There was no way he could get at it. He thumped the door in frustration. 'Anyone would think you were talking about what flavour ice cream you wanted instead of talking about what way we're going to die. We're going to die!' He turned around. 'Don't you understand? In a short while we'll be history and Miriam will be married to that disgusting old codger ...'

'Shut up, Harry,' something finally snapped in Latisha. 'Shut up!' She laid into him with her fists flying. 'I can't stand this. We're going to die. I know we're going to die! What are we to do? What do you want us to do?'

Harry held her hands to stop her hitting him any more. He drew in his breath sharply as he watched Latisha, cool, confident, dependable Latisha sink into the panic that they'd all been trying so hard to hold back.

'Easy, Lat.' He put his long, skinny arm awkwardly around her shoulder as she fell limp against him. She was shaking. Ralph and Lou looked on sympathetically. There was nothing they could say. There were no words to bring consolation to a situation so deadly desperate as this.

'At least I'll take off our chains now,' Harry said when Latisha had quietened down. The others nodded. Taking the piece of wire, he quickly manipulated each of the manacles.

'When they come for us,' Lou said quietly. 'Let's just give them all we've got.'

Latisha was beginning to regain her composure. She was taking deep breaths to prevent the short, sharp gasps of hyperventilation from overcoming her. The four of them froze as the clanking of the withdrawing mirrors cut into the silence.

Miriam began to pace the room. She looked with disgust at the lace gown that had been laid across the back of a chair. She would not put it on. She would delay everything for as long as possible. The singing was getting on her nerves. She could imagine them in there, the last of the Dwellers, sitting in rows looking up at Elder Samuel as he preached his over-the-top, lunatic beliefs at them.

She went to the window and looked down at the deserted street. The mirrors were folded and the only light came from a few lanterns which made the street appear like the deserted set of a ghostly play. She turned up the wick of the lamp and, as she did so, she remembered the amazing reaction of the two women to the light. If only she had a strong light, she thought. If only she had a powerful light that she could shine in the eyes of the Dwellers and blind them. She swayed back and forth on her feet as she thought. Light. Strong light. She looked desperately around the room and let out a breath of frustration. Turning the wick up to its fullest would hardly overpower the whole community. She looked at the yellow flame through the glass mantle. The singing had stopped. Very soon now the Dwellers would emerge onto the street in a ghoulish procession. Her time was almost up. As she sighed again, the flame flickered in a little dance.

'That's it!' She almost knocked over the lamp with her excitement. Fire! Fire was the closest she could get to bright light. If she caused a fire it would create a diversion. They'd have to fight it. They couldn't allow fire to take hold; not down here they couldn't. She gathered up the clothes on the chair and the bedclothes, making a pile in the middle of the floor. Then, muttering a quiet prayer, she took the mantle from the lamp and held the flame to the clothes. Apart from slight singeing, nothing happened. 'They're damp!' she gasped, 'the stupid things are damp!' Outside she could hear voices as people began to leave the meeting house. She looked at the wisps of smoke barely visible from the scorched clothes. In desperation, she emptied the container of oil or paraffin, she couldn't distinguish the smell - she just hoped it was highly inflammable.

At first nothing happened and she almost sobbed with anger and frustration. 'Come on, come on,' she clenched her fists. With a sudden whoosh, the clothing caught fire. 'Oh, thank you God!' Miriam gasped. Taking down dusty prints and curtains, she threw them on the fire. She pulled the bed closer so that it would catch fire too. By now she was coughing from the smoke, but didn't hesitate in her search for fuel. The dry wood of the old chair soon added to the blaze. Miriam shielded her face with her arm as she threw books and papers, in fact anything she could lay hands on, into the gathering bonfire. She felt satisfaction in seeing that the wooden interior was about to be consumed in the blaze. It was time to get out. Time to cause panic. She tried to force the window, but it was well and truly locked. With dismay she realised that her exit was cut off. Her eyes were smarting and she spluttered through the choking fumes. She couldn't get to the door and the window was held fast.

Was this it? Was this how it was going to end? She thought of the others, her friends, her brother and the other children. If this didn't work, they would be the ones to suffer. The flames were licking the end of her dress and the intense heat was terrifying. Holding her hands to her mouth, Miriam shrank against the window. She lifted her foot, glad of her Docs, and with a forceful kick, broke the window. The smoke billowed out into the street. 'Fire!' she spluttered 'fire!'

Because she was engrossed in kicking the window to get

out fast, Miriam was only barely aware of the panic among the Dwellers. Self-preservation took precedence over wedding or prisoners as they ran to get buckets of water. Elder Samuel was shouting orders at the men to form a water chain from the river, making a line to pass buckets from one to the other. If the fire got hold, then all the old wooden houses would go up like dry kindling. When she leapt to the ground, her Victorian dress torn and singed, Miriam paused only an instant to take in the confusion. She saw Elder Samuel, in his wedding suit, urging a group of bucket-carrying people towards the river. Everyone was shouting and everyone was involved in the fight against the fire.

Without delay, she slipped around the back of the blazing house and made her way to Elder Samuel's. With a quick glance around, she darted inside. Where to begin to look for the keys? She glanced desperately around the living room, the flickering flames from outside casting rippling shadows on the walls. No keys. She ran into what she presumed to be the bedroom, but it was some sort of study with thick books piled high. There were voices outside.

'Save the books!' someone cried. 'Save the records!'

Records? Of course, Miriam realised that they meant the records of the Dwellers. Naturally they would be in Elder Samuel's possession. That meant that someone was coming in here. She looked frantically about and saw another door off the study. Please let them be here. She found herself in a small bedroom with a patchwork quilt laid on the bed. A woman's nightdress was draped over it. With a jolt she realised that this must be meant for her. But there was no time to think of that now. She almost cried out when she saw the hoop of keys hanging on a nail beside the bed. She just had time to grab them before footsteps clumped into the other room. She dived under the bed, her heart thumping wildly as she waited for the footsteps to stop. Would they ever stop running in and out for the books?

When at last they stopped, she eased herself out. She looked towards the window and was gratified to see that the fire had gathered momentum. She turned up the high collar of her dress to hide her short hair and help her mingle unnoticed with the fire-fighting Dwellers. She hadn't much time. Their efficiency meant that they would eventually get the fire under control - they'd obviously had to deal with fire before. The chain of people from the river were passing buckets with great speed. Others were retrieving things from the houses nearest to the fire. Everyone had a function. Miriam watched for a moment from the side of Elder Samuel's house. Then she darted over to the detention house, grateful that the door didn't face onto the street. She peered in through the grille. Four startled faces looked out at her.

'The keys,' she gasped, 'I've got the keys.'

Twenty

'It's Miriam!' exclaimed Latisha, rushing to the grille. 'Miriam, how did ...'

Miriam put her finger to her lips.

'No time,' she hissed, as she fumbled with the keys. 'Jeez, Harry. I don't know which of these opens the lock!'

'Give them here,' said Harry. She passed them through the grille and he cast an expert eye over the bunch of old-fashioned, iron keys and isolated one. 'Here, try this one.'

Miriam tried to get it into the heavy padlock, but it wouldn't go. She was feeling desperate. Any second now she could be missed. She thrust the hoop through the grille again, and again Harry isolated a key.

'But Miriam, where can we go?' asked Lou. 'You're great to get the keys, but if we get out where can we go?'

'The way we came.' Miriam's words came out in a rush. 'I know,' she went on before Lou could mention the explosion. 'I know. But I remember a patch of sky when we ran back that time. There's a slight opening left. It's our only chance, but it's all we've got. Don't ask questions. No time.'

Lou nodded. Ralph spoke from the window which looked out onto the street. 'They're still fighting the blaze,' he said. 'They've brought up a cart with earth in it and some of them are shovelling it onto the fire. Miriam, did you cause that ...?'

'Yes. Tell you later. Oh thank goodness!' she let out a sigh of relief as the key turned.

Ralph was still at the window. 'Wait,' he said. 'Don't charge out onto the street. There's an alley behind this house. It leads almost to the stairs. If we can ...'

'The children!' put in Miriam. 'We've got to get the children! They're locked into a house on the other side.'

'Yes, of course,' agreed Ralph. 'I'd almost forgotten.' He glanced out the window again and quickly assessed the situation. 'Miriam, you must get across the street to the house where they're kept. In that get-up you mightn't be noticed. Like this place, the door is at the side, so you might be lucky. Here,' he took the keys from Harry and handed them to her. 'You'll just have to try all of them. Then get the children around the back of the house - there are lots of derelict houses there - stay behind them. Nobody ever goes there. Hopefully the Dwellers will still be busy enough not to see you. But you must hurry. The only big gap is between the last house and the stairs. You'll have to make a dash across to the stairs. We'll be watching from the alleyway. As soon as we see you, we'll make a dash too.'

'Will I come too?' asked Lou.

Miriam shook her head. 'You'd be spotted in your modern clothes,' she said. Once again, she was on her own. Harry gave her a thumbs-up as she turned away. She emerged from the side of the detention house and took in the scene across the street. The flames were leaping into the air, sparks flying in all directions as the earth and water were thrown on them. Miriam scooped up a handful of earth and smeared her face; with a bit of luck she'd blend in with the smoke-begrimed Dwellers. With her heart pounding, she eased her way along the street, pausing every so often to pick up something salvaged and put it on a pile - as if she were part of the team. Every second she expected to feel a hand on her shoulder or hear someone shout out her presence. But everyone was too engrossed in saving the village.

When she reached the house where the children were, she slipped across the smoky street and around the side. She leaned against the wall for a second to calm herself before attempting to unlock the door. She wished Harry were here, but that would have meant instant recognition. Stay cool, she told herself. Cool.

After the fourth attempt, the door opened. Most of the children were standing on a table, looking out at the excitement.

'Miriam!' Ed turned and jumped down when he saw his sister.

Miriam put her hand to her mouth and shook her head

to silence him. At least the children were awake, thank goodness for that.

'We didn't drink that stuff, like you said,' Ed whispered, pointing to the beakers on a tray. 'Except for Robert. He drank it.' Miriam groaned as he pointed to a small boy sprawled across one of the beds. He was sound asleep. By now the other children had gathered around Miriam. Including the sleeping child, there were four boys and four girls as well as Ed, all aged around seven or eight.

From her clothes they thought Miriam was another Dweller and they regarded her with silent hostility. There was not much time for explanation, so Miriam knelt down to whisper quick instructions. The children were in their nightclothes and, with a gasp of dismay Miriam saw that their feet were bare. But there would be no time to dress.

'Listen,' she said. 'We're going to get out of here, do you understand? You must follow me and you mustn't make a sound. Is that clear? No matter what you see, you must make no sound or we'll all be locked up again.'

'She's my sister,' added Ed. 'She's going to save us.'

Miriam tried to rouse Robert, but he simply grunted. 'Oh dammit,' swore Miriam. There was no point in trying to waken him. She picked up the sleeping child and went towards the door where the others stood expectantly.

'Okay?' she whispered. The children nodded. With a deep breath, Miriam led them around behind the house. As Ralph had said, there were derelict houses. She led the children behind these and urged them in the direction of the stairs. They could hear the shouts of the Dwellers and could feel the heat of the burning house as they drew near to the back of it.

'Keep down very low,' she said. Robert was a dead weight and her back felt like it would break. She pushed the hoop of keys up the length of her arm so that she could better support the sleeping boy. Now the heat and the sparks were very close. The smoke was everywhere, blinding, choking smoke, but Miriam was grateful for it.

One of the children reacted with a startled cry as some sparks landed on the pile of timber which concealed them.

Miriam closed her eyes, waiting for an outcry, but the child's shout had been lost in the general noise. She nodded to the children and led them behind the next derelict house.

One of the children began to complain that his feet hurt.

'Shut up!' Miriam hissed. 'Make a sound and we're all done for.' She was sorry when she saw the child's terrified face, but she knew there was no time for cossetting.

Now they were at the last house. Miriam peeped out. She saw Lou watching out for her from behind the detention house across the way. Now both groups were the same distance from the stairs, like two sides of a triangle. There was nothing to conceal them between here and there; it was a no-man's land of smooth earth. Could they possibly all make a dash for it and not be seen? Would they get so far only to ...? No, it didn't bear thinking about.

Lou saw her and nodded. That was the signal. No time for guesswork.

'Now,' Miriam whispered to the children. 'Make for those stairs and don't stop for anything!'

Suddenly they were all moving, Miriam, the children and Lou and the others. Knowing that they were racing for their lives gave extra speed to their feet. They all reached the stairs together and huddled at the bottom, pounding hearts and panting breath. Lou nodded again and pointed upwards. In single file, and keeping as low as possible, they began their ascent. Harry had taken the sleeping child from Miriam and she rubbed her shoulder to ease the ache caused by bearing the dead weight. On the first landing, they looked back warily. The fire was coming under control. No time to delay. When they reached the door through which they'd come - it seemed like an eternity ago - Lou took the child as Harry took the keys from Miriam. He was just trying the second key when the cry went up from below.

Twenty-One

Miriam gasped as she saw the upturned face of Elder Samuel peering through the smoke. With a group of the most robust men, he left the firefighting group and advanced in the direction of the stairs.

'They've seen us!' exclaimed Lou. 'Hurry up, Harry.'

'Stupid old locks,' muttered Harry. 'There, gotcha!'

The door squeaked open and the group of youngsters filed into the dark tunnel. Miriam, Latisha and Ralph each had children clinging to them. Lou shifted Robert onto his shoulders and carried him like he'd seen firemen do in films.

'Go on, you lot,' Harry shouted. 'I'll lock the door. That'll hold them off for a while.'

'Harry ...' began Latisha. 'They might get here before you get to lock ...'

'Go on!' Harry hissed.

It was pitch black and they had to feel their way along the rough tunnel.

'Mind your heads,' warned Lou. 'Remember this is low.'

Low, thought Miriam as she squeezed the hand of one of the frightened children. Low and narrow and black. She tried to swallow back her panic, but there was no spit. There was also no time for panic. The only thing that mattered was for all of them to get to that opening. She concentrated on trying to remember the size of the opening. Had it been big enough to see several stars, or was she clinging to an impossible dream? Was she putting too much hope in what might turn out to be a mere pinhole through which nobody could fit?

It was now so narrow that they had to go in single file. Some of the children lost the grasp of the hands they'd been holding and began to panic.

'Hold on to the clothes of the person in front of you,' Lou's muffled voice came from ahead. His voice was reassuring and Latisha realised that something normal would have to be done to keep the children going.

110

'Ten green bottles hanging on the wall,' her voice was croaky and out of tune as she sang. 'Ten green bottles hanging on the wall, come on kids, sing!'

Miriam was impressed. Trust practical Latisha to come up with a good idea at a time like this. She joined in the singing and, hesitantly at first, the children began to sing too. Then another loud raucous voice joined in from the rear and everyone knew that Harry had caught up.

'Did you get the door locked?' asked Latisha. She was last in the line and reached back to touch Harry. He gave her arm a pat. 'Sure did,' he said.

But, over the forced singing, the dull thump of something crashing against the door could be heard.

'Move faster, folks,' called Lou.

The singing was now sporadic as, several times, the line was held up when someone stumbled. Suddenly there was a cry as everyone crashed together. 'The other door,' called Lou.

'Is it locked?' shouted Harry.

Lou tried turning the handle. It was stiff at first, but slowly it began to budge. 'Help me push,' Lou said to the children nearest to him.

They groped their way forward and pushed, their bare feet slipping on the stony floor. There was a gust of dusty air as the door opened. They were now in the tunnel where the blast had been.

'Left, everyone,' shouted Lou. 'Hold hands again and turn left.'

Please let the opening be big enough, prayed Miriam. And please let the sky be bright enough for us to see it. There were so many factors weighed against them. And all of these youngsters were here because she had a blurred memory of seeing a bit of sky. She might even have imagined it! In the desperation of that moment when hands were grabbing her, she might have imagined that she saw the sky. If this goes wrong, she thought, it will be all my fault.

As they stumbled over the stony rubble caused by the explosion, the dull thud, thud of the door being battered

111

far back in the other tunnel reached their ears. The children were crying out in pain as the rough stones cut their bare feet.

'Please,' Latisha urged them. 'Please just hold out for a little longer.'

'Is everyone here?' shouted Lou. In the dark it was impossible to know who was where. Miriam knew that Latisha was behind her with two of the children. Harry brought up the rear. She herself had two children by the hand and Ed was clutching her dress. Ralph was ahead with two more children and Lou was carrying Robert and another small one was clutching his belt.

'Call out your names,' Latisha shouted. 'Starting at the back with Harry, call out your names as we move. As soon as you hear the person behind you say their name, you call out yours.'

'Harry,' 'Latisha,' 'Michael,' 'Jane,' 'Kevin,' 'Alice,' Miriam.'

'Ed,' 'Joe,' 'Tessa,' 'Angela.'

'Fine,' said Lou. 'And me, Lou. And I have whatsisname. That seems to be ...'

'Ralph!' shouted Harry. 'Where's Ralph?'

'He's here,' a small voice cried out. 'He won't get up.'

Latisha pushed ahead the children who'd been holding her and tried to locate the voice of the child who'd spoken.

'Keep talking,' she said. Harry had caught up with her and the two of them felt around in the dark. Latisha's hand fell on a curly head.

'He's here,' the child said. 'He just fell.'

Harry felt for Ralph and found him stretched against the side of the tunnel. With Latisha's help, he propped him into a sitting position. He was gasping for breath.

'Ralph! Ralph, what is it? Are you hurt?'

Now there was confusion as all the youngsters congregated together in the tiny space. A crush of bodies pressed around where Latisha and Harry were crouched over Ralph.

Harry raised his head and looked up, even though he could see no one.

'Keep going,' he said. 'Miriam, you and Lou take the kids the rest of the way. Latisha and I will take Ralph.'

'Are you sure ...?' began Miriam.

'Go on,' hissed Harry.

Miriam and Lou gathered the rest of the group. With Lou in front and herself at the back, they pressed ahead through the tunnel which was becoming rougher and stonier with each step. The singing had stopped. There was something else too. Some other noise was missing.

'The thumping,' she shouted to Lou. 'The thumping has stopped.'

A feeling of dread overcame her as she realised what this meant. The Dwellers were through.

'Maybe they've given up,' said Lou. Miriam knew he said this for the benefit of the children.

'Maybe,' she said. She turned her head and called back, 'Are you folks okay?'

Latisha's voice came from very far back. 'We're coming,' she shouted. She and Harry were supporting the almost dead weight of Ralph.

'Leave me,' his voice came in a hoarse whisper. 'Leave me. Let me lie down ...'

'Cool it, brother,' said Harry. 'We'll get you out.'

'No,' whispered Ralph. 'They won't harm me. I've been down here so long they need me - the generator. Go on, you two. I told you I was feeble,' he gave a laugh that sounded like a snort. 'I haven't run for years.' His voice was gasping and his bony body was limp. Latisha took a firmer hold around his waist.

'Come on, Ralph. You know we won't leave you. Try to move. Come on.'

She reached across to Harry and gently poked him to get his attention as she heard distant voices back in the tunnel. Harry got the message. With a mighty heave, he half carried Ralph and they made their way along the difficult path after the others.

'I see it!' cried Miriam. She had been stumbling along looking upwards for the opening that might or might not be there. 'Look. There it is.'

113

They had been climbing over rocks as the spot where the explosion had been drew nearer. Now they were at the actual place. Lou looked up. Sure enough, away up at the top of the tunnel, a narrow opening revealed the navy blue of the night sky. There was just enough light filtering through to show a high pile of loose rocks and rubble that seemed to go all the way to the top.

'I was right,' Miriam said. 'Thank God I was right.'

The children began talking at once. 'Are we there? Are we getting out? Are we going to climb up there?'

'Shush,' said Lou. 'We haven't much time. Miriam, where are you? I'll go ahead up the pile of rubble and try to find a way to the opening. You kids come after me. Miriam will be behind you. Now, remember, you must move quickly. Keep that opening in sight and try to keep in line with the way I go.'

Miriam waited until the last child went before her up the steep incline. She peered into the inky blackness for any sign of Latisha, Harry and Ralph.

'Latisha,' she shouted.

'We're here.' Thank goodness, thought Miriam. The voices were much nearer. She waited until she heard the stumbling footsteps and edged forward to meet them.

'This is it,' she said. 'This is the opening. What's wrong with Ralph?'

'Exhaustion,' said Latisha. 'Miriam, we've got to move quickly. We could hear voices.'

'Come on,' put in Harry. 'Let's get going up to this opening. If you two girls go ahead of me and support Ralph from the back, I'll push him from behind. Okay?'

With much wheezing and gasping, Ralph did his best to crawl up the rocky incline. Ahead, Lou was finding footholds in the rock that would form a path for everyone. Progress was slow and every so often someone would slip and knock the line of climbers back a few steps. Miriam and Latisha were pulling Ralph up by his arms and Harry took his weight at the back. Ralph was now and then overcome by fits of coughing.

'You're a wreck, Ralph,' gasped Latisha. 'A total wreck.

What you need is a soft bed and a gang of people dancing attendance on you. Think of that. Think of a soft bed and being pampered. Think of it, Ralph, and pull yourself up. Come on. You can do it.'

Her coaxing helped Ralph think a bit more positively and he made superhuman efforts to push his fragile, shattered body into action.

'Oh no,' gasped Miriam as she saw faint light glow along the tunnel. 'They're coming!'

Lou had reached the top. He bit his lip with frustration as he surveyed the tiny opening. The explosion had displaced some rocks which revealed the sky, but one rock lay across the outside hole, blocking the exit for all but the tiniest body. Lou pushed at the rock with all his might, but it was impossible from the inside. He knew there was no way he could ever fit through that opening. He cried out in frustration as he pushed again with all his might. The sky seemed to be mocking him as he breathed the fresh air from outside. So near, yet not near enough. He glanced down when he heard voices and he saw the lanterns carried by the pursuing Dwellers. He gave one final, useless heave. It was no good. They were all well and truly done for.

Young Ed crawled up beside him. 'What's wrong, Lou?' he asked. 'Why don't you go through?'

Lou shook his head. 'No use, Ed. We'd never get through that opening.'

Ed put his hand up and felt the night air. 'I could, Lou,' he said, 'I could get through that.'

'There's a rock outside blocking the way out,' said Lou, brightening slightly. 'Do you think you could move that?'

Ed nodded. 'If some of the others came out with me, they could help.'

'It's worth a try,' said Lou, looking down fearfully to where the Dwellers were beginning to climb, their lanterns casting eerie shadows around the rock-strewn cave. 'Come on, then. Move really quickly.'

Ed climbed ahead of him and put his arms through. Lou

pushed him from behind and for one awful moment thought of the fate that had befallen him in the gaspipe tunnel. Was this to be the same result? He gritted his teeth and pushed harder at the small body. Then, very slightly at first, Ed began to move. Suddenly he was through with a whoop of joy. He set about trying to move the rock as Lou pushed the next child through. One by one the children were pushed out and Lou could hear them grunting as they tried to manoeuvre the rock outside. It didn't budge.

Down below him, Miriam and Latisha were urging Ralph closer to the top. The Dwellers were shouting menacingly as they struggled up the slope. Harry stopped and yelled up to the girls to keep going.

'Harry!' shouted Latisha. 'Harry don't do any heroic stuff. Come on.'

Harry gave her a quick thumbs-up sign before picking up loose rocks and tossing them down on the pursuers. That stopped them, but only for a moment. They fanned out on the slope, forming an arc under Harry. There was no way that tossing stones would deter all of them.

'Harry!' the two girls shouted.

Harry turned to follow them up, but lost his footing and cried out as he felt himself slip. He looked up in desperation at the others. Latisha was reaching down for him. At the top of the pile, Lou was pushing the youngsters out, his bare, skinny chest gleaming with sweat and, around his neck that ridiculous dog whistle.

Dog whistle! Harry almost stumbled again as he thought of Lou's whistle.

'The whistle,' he shouted up to Latisha. 'Tell Lou to give me his whistle!'

'What ...?'

'The whistle. Pass down the goddam whistle.'

Lou heard him from above, puzzled at first, but then realisation dawned on him. He whipped the whistle from around his neck and reached down to Miriam's outstretched hand. Miriam still didn't know what was going on, but this was not a time to ask questions. She quickly passed it to Latisha. Harry cried out as one of the

116

Dwellers grasped his foot and tried to pull him down. Latisha slithered over the rocks and handed the whistle to Harry. She could see him being pulled away and tried to catch his other arm. Harry blew on the whistle with all his might as he tried to kick away the Dweller. Others were now closing in. He almost cried out in frustration. The blasted whistle made no sound. The pathetic thing didn't work! He was about to throw it at his pursuers when he felt the grip on his foot loosen. When he looked, all the men below were clutching their ears. Their super hearing, as sharp as that of a dog, had picked up whatever sound came from the whistle.

Harry swiftly found his footing and followed the others up the rocky slope.

As Lou pushed the last small child through, there was a cheer as the outside rock began to move.

'We've got it,' shouted Ed. 'We've moved it!'

Harry cast one last look below as he reached the opening. The Dwellers had recovered and were making their way up again.

'Go on you,' he shouted to Lou who was waiting to help him through. Turning around, he gave one more blast on the whistle. Without waiting to see the consequences, Lou swung himself up to where the girls were waiting to grab him. Then Harry gave a cry of relief as eager hands also pulled him through into the cold night air.

<u>Epilogue</u>

'Is that real cream or some sort of fake stuff?' asked Miriam.

Harry stuck his finger into the white concoction which dripped between two layers of pastry and licked it.

'Shaving foam with a dash of Milk of Magnesia,' he said.

'Gross. Eat it yourself,' Miriam pushed the bun across the check paper tablecloth.

'Well I don't make the stupid things, I only serve them,' said Harry, wiping his hands on his white wrap-around apron. 'Personally, I wouldn't touch that muck if I was in the last stages of malnutrition.'

Latisha smiled. 'Still, isn't this better than spending your weekends hanging about with people of The Mob class?'

'Oh I don't know,' said Harry. 'You get to see some interesting things in sleazy places. I miss the low life.' He grinned when he saw Latisha's face grow serious. 'Yeah, well I guess you're right, Lat. Part-time waiter in a coffee shop is the first step to owning my own chain of restaurants. Now that you folks have blackmailed me into staying at school for another while, I'll be able to write my name and sign fat cheques.'

'And read the graffiti on your own lavatory walls,' said Miriam.

'Not in my restaurants,' laughed Harry. 'I'll employ ex-wrestlers to deal with any trouble-makers while I hop around in my air-conditioned limo.'

'With a bimbo on each arm,' added Latisha.

'One bimbo will do me fine,' Harry winked at Latisha who pretended to bristle.

'This bimbo will probably be your lawyer keeping you out of jail,' she laughed. 'Nothing changes.'

'Listen Mr Bigshot, I hate to cut across your business plans,' said Miriam, 'but there's a group over there waiting to be served and they are casting nasty glances over this way. If I were you I'd see to them before your boss boots you and your air-conditioned limo hopes out the door.'

Harry glanced guiltily towards the serving counter and hurried away. Lou watched Harry lope across the café and grinned. He put down the letter he had been reading and stirred his coffee.

'Great letter,' he said. 'Ralph's certainly enjoying all the fuss being made of him. Can you imagine the look on his folks' faces when the police rang them that night?'

'Will he be in hospital for long?' asked Latisha.

Lou nodded. 'Probably doing all kinds of tests and stuff,' he said. 'I'm sure he's a bit messed up inside his head as well. It'll take ages for him to adjust to the real world again. Not to mention getting used to a new brother and sister who were born while he was below.'

'He will,' said Latisha. 'Anyone who could keep sane all those years - well, he must have a superhuman brain. Ralph will be okay. He's amazing.'

'Jeez,' said Lou. 'I didn't think we'd get him out. I thought he'd pass away in that tunnel.'

'Tell me about it,' said Miriam. 'Going up those rocks I thought we were all dead meat. Isn't it funny how being scared mindless makes you able to do things you'd never think you could do? What do they call it ... ad ... addendum ...?'

'Adrenalin,' said Lou. 'It's a hormone that responds to stress ...'

Miriam smiled. 'Oh, oh. We're in for a lecture again.'

Latisha pressed her hand to her forehead dramatically. 'Oh, no. Please. Not more heavy stuff from Doctor Brains.'

Lou looked at the two girls over his new glasses. 'Why would I waste good words, I ask myself, on a couple of airheads like you? You lot should never even have got the vote.'

'Tell that to the Dwellers,' laughed Latisha. 'They'd agree.'

'Those crazies,' Miriam shuddered. 'When I think of what might have become of those kids ...'

'I hope they get over the bad times they had,' said Latisha. 'How's Ed?'

Miriam shrugged. 'He has the odd nightmare and freaks

119

out. But mostly he thinks he's some super hero. Says only for him moving that rock we'd all still be down there. Little prat.'

She didn't mention her own nightmares. Images that loomed in her sleep most nights. Images of Elder Samuel reaching out a bony hand to touch her face, his yellow teeth bared in a sickening grin. Images of a dim, deserted street set out for a bizarre wedding ritual and images of ghoulish figures that menacingly watched her from shadowy corners. And fire; it wasn't until much later that she realised that she could have perished in that fire. Her eyebrows were just beginning to grow back. She knew those nightmares would haunt her for a long time to come.

'I wonder where they are, the Dwellers,' mused Latisha. 'Should have been buried, the creeps. I hope they get put away in the slammer - even that'd be too good for them.'

'Well, they've been there,' put in Lou. 'That hell hole was worse than any slammer. No, they're all in some government hideaway being rehabilitated or brain-washed or de-briefed, whatever. Can you imagine what would happen if it leaked out where they are? There would be cameras and reporters hanging from trees. If that lot can snap the Royals in their knickers, can't you see what a pantomime they'd make of the Dwellers?'

'Well,' Latisha shuddered, 'let's hope they send them as far away as possible. I wouldn't want to meet any of that lot again. Not ever.' She pressed hard on the bun so that the cream oozed out on either side.

Miriam pursed her lips and looked thoughtful.

'What are you thinking about, Mim,' asked Lou.

'I'm thinking about those people, those Dwellers,' she said.

'Creeps,' said Latisha.

'Maybe,' murmured Miriam.

'Maybe!' Latisha recoiled. 'Are you out of your tree?'

'I know. I know what you're going to say,' put in Miriam, 'but ...'

'But you can't help feeling sorry for them,' said Lou.

'No, not sorry for them,' continued Miriam. 'Not really.

But I wish the world was a bit different.'

Latisha shook her head in disbelief.

'Oh I can't put it in the right words,' said Miriam with a note of exasperation. How could she describe her feelings as she thought of a gentle, frail creature like Lucy Ambrose trying to take on board the darker side of this new world?

'It's not a happy-ever-after situation, is that what you're trying to say, Mim?' asked Lou gently.

Miriam looked at him gratefully. 'That's it. They're up here now, in our world, and it's not such a brilliant place.'

'Lighten up, Miriam,' said Latisha. 'They'll be well looked after.'

'I know,' said Miriam. 'But maybe they'd have been better off if they'd been left where they were. I have these strange, mixed-up nightmares where I'm either trapped below with them or else they're undergoing awful tests up here. You see,' she looked at the others, 'one nightmare doesn't cancel out the other.'

'Oh, Miriam,' said Latisha, sympathetically.

'It's okay, it's okay,' said Miriam. 'If I could laugh at it, the nightmares would probably go away. Don't go treading easily around me, please. I couldn't bear that. I'd feel like some loony that has to be humoured.'

Lou looked at her intently for a moment, still holding her hand.

'You are some loony who has to be humoured,' he said, 'a loony who almost got fried trying to save us all,' he entwined his fingers through hers. 'A loony we owe our necks to.'

His new glasses made him look more grown-up and he'd taken to wearing more modern gear since he had become a high-profile survivor. Miriam looked at the freckle-backed hand that was holding hers and felt a warm glow inside.

'Is this your biker?' Mum had whispered when she had first brought him home.

'I'm working on it,' she had whispered back with a grin.

Miriam suddenly shrank low in her seat as the door of the café swung open. 'Don't look now,' she whispered, 'but isn't that the woman reporter that called into the school last Wednesday?'

Lou groaned. 'Oh no. I've had it up to here with reporters and telly interviews and my mug splashed on the Sunday heavies. It's all old news now. Can't they give us a break?'

Latisha was smiling. 'No fear of Harry being fed up with publicity,' she said. 'Look at him.'

Harry had recognised the reporter and was making his way towards her with that special 'publicity' smile he was cultivating.

'That's our Harry, Showman Extraordinaire,' laughed Lou. 'He's probably working on the film rights! Let's nip away and leave him to it.'

Bright Sparks

The King & I and the Rest of the Class
by Lucy Mitchell

When the principal of St Mary's Girl's School announces that the Transition Year students will be staging *The King & I* with the boys from St Patrick's, Aoife and her best friends, Brenda, Emma and Elaine are thrilled ... 'Boyfriends for Christmas.'
Aoife wants a cool boyfriend with the right jeans and trendy trainers. The King has caught everybody's eye with his stunning good looks and his rapid sucession of girlfriends. But when Aoife finds out that Brian - a friendly, intelligent stage-hand and the owner of a pair of drastic runners - fancies her, she finds herself asking if she should try to put his personality before his appearance.

Price: £4.99
ISBN: 1 85594 138 4

Bright Sparks

Daisy Chain War
by Joan O'Neill

Set during the late thirties and forties, this is a heartwarming story of cousins, Irish Lizzie and English Vicky, growing up during 'The Emergency'.

'An eye-opener for the young reader and a nostalgic treat for the older one.'

Robert Dunbar *The Irish Times*

Price: £4.99
ISBN: 1 85594 004 3

Bright Sparks

After the Famine
by Colette McCormack

The famine years are hard for Mary-Anne to forget, but now she is building a life for herself in the new world. New York offers a lot to a young girl - but there are also strange and unknown dangers facing the immigrants crowded into the hazardous, hellish sweatshops of the city ...
And then Sean Thornton, her beloved schoolmaster, is beginning to realise that Mary-Anne is no longer a little girl ... But what about Tim O'Connor, the handsome, young policeman she is walking out with? And the wealthy Janine?

Price: £4.99
ISBN: 1 85594 142 2

Bright Sparks

The Rocket Girl
by Caroline Barry

The Rocket Girl lives in Rocket Castle in the town of Mecklenstarr, home to a wonderful array of extraordinary characters. In the Castle itself live Aristotle, the talking, philosophising cat, Uncle Jeremiah Fine, the inventor, the Rocket Girl and her new-found friend, Shape, the demon.

Together with the mysterious Count Evelli they must save Mecklenstarr and its inhabitants from corruption and cruelty in the form of the Earl of Copperfelt and his henchman, the Bishop. With a concoction of magic, wit and imagination they must overcome the forces of evil and ensure that the Rocket Girl can claim her inheritance - Rocket Castle.

Price: £4.99
ISBN: 1 85594 143 0

THE BRIGHT SPARKS FAN CLUB

WOULD YOU LIKE TO JOIN?

Would you like to receive a **FREE** bookmark and BRIGHT SPARKS friendship bracelet?

You are already halfway there. If you fill in the questionnaire on the next page and one other questionnaire from the back page of any of the other BRIGHT SPARKS titles and return both questionnaires to Attic Press at the address below, you automatically become a member of the BRIGHT SPARKS FAN CLUB.

If you are, like many others, a lover of the BRIGHT SPARKS fiction series and become a member of the BRIGHT SPARKS FAN CLUB, you will receive special discount offers on all new BRIGHT SPARKS books, plus a BRIGHT SPARKS bookmark and a beautiful friendship bracelet made with the BRIGHT SPARKS colours. Traditionally friendship bracelets are worn by friends until they fall off! If your friends would like to join the club, tell them to buy the books and become a member of this book lovers' club.

Please keep on reading and spread the word about our wonderful books. We look forward to hearing from you soon.

Name _____

Address _____

_____

Age _____

For a catalogue of all books in the Bright Sparks series or to order individual titles, you can post, fax, phone or E-mail us direct at:
Attic Press, 29 Upper Mount St, Dublin 2, Ireland.
Tel: (353 1) 661 6128 Fax: (353 1) 661 6176
E-mail: Atticirl@iol.ie   http://www.iol.ie/~atticirl/

Attic Press hopes you enjoyed *The Dwellers Beneath*. To help us improve the **Bright Sparks** series for you please answer the following questions.

1. Why did you decide to buy this book?

_____

_____

_____

2. Did you enjoy this book? Why?

_____

_____

_____

3. Where did you buy it?

_____

_____

_____

4. What do you think of the cover?

_____

_____

_____

5. Have you ever read any other books in the **BRIGHT SPARKS** series? Which one/s?

_____

_____

_____

6. Have you any comments to make on the books in the **BRIGHT SPARKS** series?

_____

_____

_____

If there is not enough space for your answers on this coupon please continue on a sheet of paper and attach it to the coupon.

Post this coupon to **Attic Press**, 29 Upper Mount Street, Dublin 2 and we'll send you a **BRIGHT SPARKS** bookmark.

Name_____Age_____
Address _____
_____Date_____

For a catalogue of all books in the Bright Sparks series or to order individual titles, you can post, fax, phone or E-mail us direct at:
Attic Press, 29 Upper Mount St, Dublin 2, Ireland.
Tel: (353 1) 661 6128 Fax: (353 1) 661 6176
E-mail: Atticirl@iol.ie   http://www.iol.ie/~atticirl/